EDA BLESSED III

Milton J. Davis

MVmedia, LLC Fayetteville, GA

MVmedia, LLC
PO Box 143052
Fayetteville, GA 30214
www.mvmediaatl.com

Publisher's Note: This is a work of fiction. Names, characters, places, and incidents are a product of the author's imagination. Locales and public names are sometimes used for atmospheric purposes. Any resemblance to actual people, living or dead, or to businesses, companies, events, institutions, or locales is completely coincidental.

Eda Blessed III / Milton J. Davis. -- 1st ed.
ISBN 979-8-9905121-6-0

To Ronald T. Jones. Sword and Soul Forever.

CONTENTS

The Escape

Omari woke to a gentle tugging of his left foot. A grin formed on his stubbled face as the image of the woman he'd taken to bed formed in his thoughts, although he couldn't recall her name. There had been quite a few over the past two weeks, and his head was still a bit fuzzy from too much palm wine and beer.

The pulling became stronger, and he cracked his eyes open. A broad figure, its face hidden by a thick scarf, gripped his boot. Omari's head cleared; the pleasure fog replaced by anger. He was being robbed.

"Get away from him," a gruff voice called out. "We're not here for shoes. We're here for stacks."

"Speak for yourself," the man holding Omari's foot retorted. "These are Malian sand boots. They'll fetch a fortune in the market, but these are destined for my feet."

"No, they're not," Omari said.

The thief's eye widened. Omari jerked his left leg to his chest while kicking out with his right, smashing his sole into the thief's face. The hapless man fell onto his back, unconscious with a shattered nose.

Omari rose to his knees, looking for his swords.

"It's him!" one of the thieves shouted.

Omari rolled from the mattress onto another sleeping companion. Struggling to his feet, a wave of dizziness gripped him, and he stumbled backward, tripping over another person on his floor. When he stood again, the thieves were advancing on him, daggers in their hands.

"Don't kill him!" the thief in the center of the advancing line said. "At least not until we find where the stacks are hidden."

Omari charged at the man. The other thieves converged on him, but he reached their leader first. He exposed his torso, hoping the thief would lunge for his stomach. He did. Omari rose on the ball of his right foot then spun away, grabbing the man's wrist at the same time. He drove his fist into the man's jaw then snatched the knife from his weakened grip.

Omari dodged the other thieves then sprinted toward the door. He was beginning to smile when a massive, masked man stepped into the portal, a dagger in each hand.

"Daarila's beard!" Omari snarled.

He increased his pace, lifting the stolen dagger over his head. The big brute raised his arms, preparing for the attack. At the last moment, Omari dropped low then rammed his right shoulder into the man's soft gut, wrapping his arms around the man's waist then lifting him off his feet. The man struck down with his daggers, driving them into Omari's back. He winced as his ngisimaugi, his healing tattoo, flared. The tangled duo hit the weak railing, hesitating just a moment before the wood cracked and they fell three stories to the street below.

The big man hit the stone with a loud crack. Omari bounced off him, then landed beside the dead man on his chest, knocking the wind out of him. He scrambled to his feet as he tried to breathe, looking like a tigerfish dragged out of the river. The other bandits clambered down the stairs, knives at the ready. Omari remembered the blades in his back; unfortunately, he couldn't reach them.

"Cleave!" he wheezed.

His breath returned as the men reached him. Omari rolled onto his left side, careful not to push the knives deeper into his back. He kicked the first man to reach him on his shin, then caught him as he fell on top of him. Omari snatched the knife from the man's hand, then rolled him aside with a slit throat. He jumped to his feet and the last two bandits stopped, uncertainty on their faces.

"Leave and live," Omari hissed.

The men looked at each other, turned on their heels, and fled. Omari remained in his stance until he was sure the men didn't intend to double back, then let out a sigh and began the painful journey back to his room, ignoring the stares and whispers of the gathering crowd. A young woman with a basket balanced on her head broke from the crowd to walk with him. She stood almost as tall as Omari and had a pleasant face and wide smile.

"You're naked," she said.

Omari glanced at the woman. "I am."

"Why?"

Omari chuckled. "Some things are better this way."

The woman smiled. "You have knives in your back. Would you like me to remove them?"

"Yes, please."

"It will hurt."

"No worse that it hurts now."

Omari stopped walking as the woman put down her bundle. He hissed through his gritted teeth as she removed the knives. A moment later he felt a hand run across his lower back.

"Is there a knife there, too?" he asked.

"No," the woman replied. "Your tattoo is glowing."

"It does that sometimes."

The woman walked beside him again, the pain subsiding as the ngisimaugi did its work. She handed him the knives. Although his attackers were bandits, they had good taste in blades. At least whomever they stole them from did. Omari gave the knives back to her.

"Keep them," Omari said. "Consider it payment. They should sell for a good price."

"Thank you," the woman replied. She reached up and dropped the knives in her basket. "I hope the rest of your day is better. Eda bless."

"Eda bless," Omari replied.

By the time he reached the top of the stairs his wounds had healed. The revelers slept through the entire incident, not that they would have been any help. He trudged over to his bed, realizing that it was time to leave the Cape and begin his journey home to Sati-Baa. He donned his clothes, secured his weapons then walked across the room to the secret compartment he had built into the wall. He took out the loosened stone, revealing the satchel with his payment from the Kamites. He counted the contents and groaned. Meresankh's words were prophetic. Omari had spent half his stacks. However, what remained still made him a wealthy man. But he couldn't carry them around, nor could he leave the city with them without being noticed. This burglary meant he was a marked man. If he hired bodyguards, he wouldn't be able to trust them, and if he left the city alone, he'd surely be followed. Omari laughed; he finally knew what it felt like to be a target of someone like him. There was an alternative, one that made his mouth turn sour. He immediately reconsidered. If he left during the night, he might be able to leave the city unnoticed. He would have to change his dwelling first. He was sure his current residence was being watched.

"Omari?"

He turned to see one of the women in his bed rise and rub her eyes. He took in her beauty and felt his loins stir. A sultry smile came to her groggy face.

"Where are you going?" she asked.

"For a walk," he replied.

She blinked away her sleepiness then studied him.

"You're not coming back, are you?"

"No, I'm not," Omari confessed.

"Then take me with you."

"I can't do that," he said. "Last night was wonderful, but it was last night."

"Then at least give me one last kiss," she said.

Omari knew he was in for more than a kiss, but he decided there was nothing wrong with that. He sauntered to the bed then knelt on the mattress. The woman wrapped one arm around his neck, then pressed a dagger to his throat with the other.

"If you want to live, you'll . . ."

Omari jerked free from the woman's embrace then punched her across the jaw before she could finish her sentence. She dropped to the bed unconscious.

"By the Cleave!" Omari exclaimed.

He ran out of the room, down the stairs then merged into the morning crowd. Omari's eyes darted from side to side as worry filled his gut. Everyone looked suspicious to him. He couldn't trust anyone. He couldn't wait until tonight to leave; he needed this pressure off his shoulders immediately, even if it meant half his fortune. What would remain would still be enough to do what he wished for when he finally made it back to Sati-Baa.

10

He made his way to the merchant district. The people he sought would be there, if anywhere. Whether or not they would help him was another matter. He strolled through the ward, stopping only for a quick meal of dried goat and bread. The buildings became larger and more refined as he neared the docks, for the wealthier merchants lived close to their livelihoods. The whitewashed walls and red ceramic roofs reminded Omari of Kiswala. He wasn't interested in such homes; his destination would be much less obvious.

He turned the corner down a road that ran parallel to the shore. This was where the warehouses were located, plain stone buildings that contained the wealth of their owners. It was there he found his destination. The two-story graystone building hid between two similar buildings. A single guard stood beside the basic cedar door, his upper body clothed in a white tunic covered by a chainmail shirt. A leather helmet protected his head. White and blue striped cotton pants covered his torso down to his knees, a pair of leather sandals on his feet. He held a spear twice his height; a curved sword rested in the worn baldric hanging from his shoulder. The man looked almost bored, but Omari knew better. The guardian's eyes narrowed as Omari neared, his hand tightening on his spear. Omari halted well out of thrusting range.

"I seek assistance from your elders," Omari said.

"By what right?" the guard asked.

"By right of brotherhood."

Omari pulled back his sleeve, revealing a portion of his ngisimaugi. The guard's eyes narrowed.

"Approach."

He passed the first test. The second test would be more difficult.

"What are you doing here, Mikijen?" the guard asked. "There are no Kiswala vessels in the harbor. Are you a deserter?"

"How can a mercenary desert what they are paid to do?" Omari replied.

"Are you on an errand?" the guard asked. "If you are, your employer is surely not Kiswalan. You are out of uniform."

"I'm here for business."

The guard chuckled. "With what?"

"This." Omari took the satchel from his shoulder then opened it. The guard peered inside. A look of interest came to his face.

"Are we stealing from our employers?" he asked. "Or are you selling chagga or kola nuts?"

"It is a payment from a Kamite client," Omari answered. "Besides, whatever I'm doing, or not doing, is none of your business. What kind of guard are you?"

The man smirked. "A cautious one. Kamites are known for being loose with their stacks. Whatever you did for them, this payment was too much."

"What does that matter?" Omari fussed. "It's mine. And besides, since when have Wabenka been concerned about where a person's wealth comes from?"

"There have been incidents," the guard said. He gave Omari a hard look for a few more minutes. "Wait here."

The guard knocked on the door. Moments later it opened and another guard appeared. The two exchanged words; the new guard replacing the other. With nothing else left to do, Omari sat before the building and finished his dried goat and bread. The day crept by, sunlight replaced by darkness. Omari still waited, leaving for food and to relieve himself. He was determined not to leave until his stacks were in safe hands. It was almost midnight when the first guard returned.

"Follow me," he said.

Omari yawned then entered. The inside of the building was as sparse as the outside, a narrow bare corridor leading to a small room with two benches before a raised desk. A woman sat behind the desk; her hair covered with a mud cloth wrap. She motioned Omari forward.

"State your name," the woman said.

"Omari Ket."

"I am Buhle. What is your reason for seeking our help?"

Omari lifted his stack bag. "I wish to deposit my stacks. I'm traveling to Sati-Baa and wish to withdraw them upon my arrival."

"You wish to safeguard your stacks for travel to Sati-Baa, Omari Ket," the woman confirmed.

"Yes," Omari replied.

"Let it be known that the man known as Omari Ket wishes to transfer his stacks to our money house in Sati-Baa."

Omari heard scribbling, but he could not pinpoint the source. The scribbling stopped.

"So noted," said a voice from beyond the room.

"You are aware of the transaction fee, are you not?"

Omari tried not to gag. "Yes."

"Let it be noted that Omari Ket has agreed to relinquish fifty percent of his total as transaction and transportation fees."

Omari's eyes went wide. "Transportation fees? My stacks aren't going anywhere. I am!"

"The Wabenkabu are not blind or deaf," the woman said. "A person who spends their wealth recklessly captures our attention. They also get the attention of others interested in acquired their wealth. Eventually, they will come to us if they survive their spending spree. We suspect that is why you are here."

Omari scowled. The woman leaned over the counter and smiled.

"Those that seek your stacks do not care if you are alive or dead when they collect them. You cannot leave the city without being seen . . . unless we assist you."

"And how will you do that?"

"You are not the first with wealth who has required a stealthy departure from a city or situation. Upon your request, we will take responsibility for getting you out of this city and on a significant way into your desired journey."

Omari rolled his eyes as he leaned on the counter. The woman glared at him and Omari sat straight.

"It is your decision," the woman said. "You have the remainder of the day to decide. If we do not hear from you before sunset, we will assume you have decided not to take our offer."

"I have to think about it," Omari said.

"As you wish," the woman said.

Omari turned to walk away.

"One more thing," the woman spoke.

Omari turned around with a snarl. "What else? You've already taken half of my money."

"We must secure you with an identification anklet."

"A what?"

"An identification anklet," the woman said again. "When you reach Sati-Baa, our bankers must have a way to identify you when you arrive to collect your stacks."

"You can send a runner dog with my likeness," Omari said.

"That is unreliable, especially at such a great distance," the woman said. "The anklet with confirm you are who you say you are."

Omari frowned. "You could use other means. I know you have them."

"Those are reserved for internal communications," the woman replied. "If you are aware of them, you also know how taxing they can be to those who convey them."

Omari had seen the Kiswala use spirit messengers when at sea. They were highly effective, but as Buhle said, the effort was brutal. It was done only when absolutely necessary because the amount of kipande required was expensive and damaging to the messenger. Most could not survive more than five sendings. He hated the idea of having something attached to his body, but if he wanted to secure his stacks, he had no choice.

"Okay, let's do it," Omari said.

Buhle nodded. "Follow me."

Omari heard a click as Buhle stood and turned away. She pressed against the seamless wall and a door appeared. Buhle walked into the darkness, not looking to see if Omari followed. He shrugged then entered a wide corridor. Rooms filled with stacks were on both sides, with men and women counting and scribbling on tablets. Omari's old instincts almost overwhelmed him; he slowed then entered one of the rooms, considering grabbing as much as he could then fleeing for his life. But he remembered what was in his satchel was more than enough. When he returned to the corridor, the woman was staring at him and shaking her head.

"Once a thief," she said.

Omari shrugged. "Old habits."

They reached a room at the end of the passageway. Unlike the others, it was bare of stacks. An old, bare-chested, brown-skinned man sat at a large table, tinkering with a metal object.

Behind him was a large forge, a fire blazing in the massive fireplace. He looked up as they entered the room.

"Wait here," Buhle said. She entered the room. "Fezile, I have work for you."

"What do you need?"

"An identification anklet."

The woman handed Fezile the parchment with Omari's information. Fezile nodded his bald head as he read it. He placed it down then looked around Buhle to Omari.

"Come in, bwana Ket," the man said.

Omari entered the room, searching for a quick exit just in case.

"Which ankle?" Fezile asked.

"Uh, what?" Omari asked.

"Which ankle for the anklet?"

Omari shrugged. "It doesn't matter."

Fezile grunted as he knelt. He took a knotted string from his pouch then wrapped it around Omari's left ankle, noting which knot gave the right measurement. He stood then ambled to his shelves, pulling out lengths of metal until he found a match. Omari watched with curiosity as Fezile placed the metal rod on the table then went to his desk. He grabbed a plain ceramic bowl containing a dark substance and wooden stylus then returned to the table. Dipping the pen into the bowl, he proceeded to write on the metal, leaving a trail of glowing blue letters.

"Kipande," Omari said.

"Not exactly," Fezile replied. "It's a secret blend, with kipande one of the ingredients, albeit the most important one. It is exclusive to us."

Fezile finished writing. He took the metal and knelt before Omari. Omari looked puzzled.

"How are you . . ."

Fezile chanted then bent the metal around his ankle.

"How does that feel?" Fezile asked.

"It feels fine."

Fezile nodded. He touched the metal ends with his fingers and the anklet sealed.

"This anklet can only be removed by my counterpart in Sati-Baa," Fezile said. "Unless someone cuts off your foot. I assume you won't allow that."

Omari squatted then grasp the anklet. He tugged at it and it didn't budge.

The woman touched him on his shoulder. "I'll show you your quarters."

"Like I said, I won't be staying," Omari replied. "When should I return?"

"In one week . . . if you can."

The woman led Omari from the innards of the building and to the streets. The sun had yet to rise, and Omari was happy for the oil streetlamps. He immediately headed for the hostels near the docks. It was the one part of the Cape where he hadn't frequented, so he was less likely to be noticed. He'd avoided the area because there wasn't much of his type of distractions, but now since he was leaving soon, he was less inclined to seek amorous company.

The enticing smell of roasted goat drew Omari to an establishment residing on a strip of land extending into the harbor. By the time Omari reached its doors, his stomach was rumbling with hunger. The business was sparsely occupied at the early hour, a scattering of people seated in dark corners. A comely woman met him at the door, smiling as she adjusted her stained apron.

"My, aren't you a handsome one," she said.

"I've been called worse," Omari replied, sharing a smile.

"Follow me," she said. "I have a special table just for you."

The woman led him to a table near the kitchen. Omari frowned; he didn't look forward to kitchen clatter ruining his meal.

"What's so special about this table?" he asked.

"You'll be served first," she replied. "And you'll be served by me."

Omari winked. "That's sounds enticing."

The woman brushed an errant braid from her face. "What will you have?"

"What's your best?"

"Anything from the sea," the woman replied. "The sea bass with lobster tails is amazing."

"I'll take it," Omari said. "And a gourd of you best beer."

"As you wish," the woman said. She glided into the kitchen. Omari took his money bag from his pouch. He'd kept enough cowries and gold dust to get him to Sati-Baa, barring any unexpected expenses. And even if he had such troubles, he knew what he needed to do to refill his bags. For ten years he traveled the width and length of Ki Khanga, hiring out his sword and other skills to make do. It was hard, but much easier than eking out a living on the streets as he did as a boy. His thoughts drifted back to those days, and Aisha's image appeared, bringing a smile to his face. He wondered what her life was like now. Was she the wife of a rich merchant? An owner of a tavern or restaurant? Or was she a merchant with a fleet of ships plying the Sati Sea? Whatever she was, wherever she was, he knew she was no longer living in the streets. She was too smart and too beautiful for that.

Omari was laughing to himself when a crowd of men entered the tavern. He immediately recognized the two he let live earlier; apparently, they hadn't learned their lesson. He stood, drawing his sword and dagger then stopped as he recognized the person the bandits surrounded. It was a sonchai.

"Shit!" he said.

He was about to sprint into the kitchen when an unseen force gripped his body and squeezed him like a giant's hand. Omari's tattoo flared at the same time and the force that held him loosened. The sonchai shook and gritted his teeth.

"Hurry!" the sonchai said with a voice as rough as sand. "He has protection!"

The bandits ran toward him just as the woman emerged from the kitchen.

"What are you . . . eeeeeekkkk!!!"

She threw his meal at the bandits then ran back into the kitchen. The slight delay was all Omari needed. The ngisimaugi broke the sonchai's grip and Omari spun around, slicing the bandits nearest to him across their torsos with both blades. A third man tried to stop but slid into Omari's sword. The other attackers, seeing that the sonchai's conjuring had failed, fled the restaurant. The sonchai raised his hands in surrender.

"Please, don't hurt me!" he pleaded. "I didn't know their plan. I was only to restrain you. They told me nothing else!"

Omari threw his knife into the sonchai's forehead then watched him fall dead onto his back.

"You should have chosen better friends," Omari said.

"Get out!"

Omari turned to see a wide man with arms as thick as his gut. The man held a cleaver in each hand, waving them as if he knew how to use them. The server woman peeked over his shoulder. Omari didn't feel threatened, but he didn't want a fight either.

"Give me my food or my money and I will," Omari replied.

The man turned to the woman. "Give me his money!"

"Hey!" she protested. "You got plenty of food back there!"

"The money!"

The woman handed the owner her pouch. He put down his cleavers then strode to Omari.

"How much?"

Omari sheathed his sword and knife then punched the owner with a right hook that knocked him to the floor unconscious.

"Nothing," he said. He smiled at the woman. "You said he had food in the back?"

The woman grinned. "Plenty."

"Then make me a plate, and feed everyone else here too," he said. Omari glanced at the owner sprawled on the floor. "I'm sure he won't mind."

The woman scurried into the kitchen and set about making meals for everyone. The other workers dragged the bandits' bodies outside then dumped them into the bay. Two of them tended to the owner while the patrons feasted. The server brought Omari a plate stacked with delectables and a plate for herself. They sat at his table and ate.

"And what's your name?" Omari asked.

"Zola," she answered.

Omari swallowed a chunk of sea bass. "I'm Omari."

"You're trouble," Zola replied.

"Sometimes," Omari said. "Tell me, Zola. Do you like trouble?"

Zola grinned as she twirled a shrimp with her fingers.

"I could be persuaded," she said. "We rent rooms. You could stay a night . . . or two."

A loud groan interrupted their banter. The owner sat up, rubbing his jaw. He swept the restaurant with narrow eyes that stopped at Omari and Zola.

"Why are these people eating my food?" he said.

"My treat," Omari replied. He tossed a pouch of gold dust to the man and he caught it. He'd have to take a withdrawal before he set sail to replace it. "That should be enough."

The owner stood. "Enough? What about the damage to my tavern?"

Omari unsheathed his sword then placed it on the table. "That should be enough."

The bravado drained from the owner's face. He snatched the pouch then stormed toward the kitchen.

"Zola, you're fired!" he shouted.

Zola jumped to her feet.

"Fired? You can't fire me. I'm your daughter!"

She ran into the kitchen after the owner. Omari cleaned his plate then left the tavern. He decided to take the Wabenkabu up on their offer. A night of peace would be perfect. He'd had too much excitement this day.

* * *

Omari woke with a stiff back. His mattress was just a tad softer than stone, and his tattered headrest had seen too many seasons. Still, it was a decent trade for a night of uninterrupted sleep. A servant came to his room to let him know breakfast was ready, and he followed him to a small dining hall. He was served a decent meal consisting of amazimba and mealie bread, with tea, which he ate alone. He was wiping his bowl with the last of his bread when Buhle came to his table.

"I hope you slept well," she said.

"I did," Omari replied. "Although I hate sleeping alone."

Buhle looked as if a bee stung her in the mouth.

"Your ship sails this morning. Finish your breakfast then follow me."

Buhle waited as Omari cleaned his bowl and drank his tea. He followed her to a stairwell that descended to a lower-level room filled with unmarked crates. Omari didn't need to guess the contents. The Wabenkabu were in the currency business, and there was no doubt of what the crates contain.

"That is your crew," Buhle said, pointing at a group of laborers taking crates stacked in the left corner and carrying them away.

"They have been told you will accompany them. Follow them to their ship and the nahoda will check you in. Safe travels, Omari Ket."

Buhle walked away before Omari could respond. He shrugged then followed the loaders out of the chamber and into a wide corridor. They walked for a time, Omari growing concerned the longer it took for them to reach the docks. It wasn't a matter of whether their destination was true, it was that he hated confined spaces. He sighed happily when he caught the scent of the sea. Sunlight breached the dimness moments later, and they exited onto a platform below the docks. The nahoda and her msaidizi inspected the cargo hold, the msaidizi making a mark on his slate for each crate. They stood the same height, almost as tall as Omari, and wore similar garb common to the mabaharia of the region; white cotton shirts gathered at the waist by black sashes and sturdy cotton pantaloons exposing their calves. Leather sandals covered their feet. The nahoda's silk headwrap decorated with gold charms reflected her rank and wealth. The duo looked up when Omari approached. The nahoda smiled, her brown face weathered yet pleasant. The bearded msaidizi's expression was neutral.

"Ket," the nahoda said as she extended her hand. "I am Lindiwe Jabavu. This — she pointed to her msaidizi — is Gugulethu Mbeki. Welcome to the *Aamhle*."

"Thank you," Omari said. "How long will it take us to reach Sati-Baa?"

"A few weeks," Lindiwe said. "We have a number of dockings before."

Omari frowned. "That's disappointing."

"We're a working vessel. Some things cannot be helped," Lindiwe said. "But you are to be treated as an honored guest, so the journey won't be too taxing."

Omari forced a smile. He knew from his time as a Mikijen that the difference between the accommodations of crew and honored guest was small. At the most, his headrest would be soft; most likely it meant his food would be heated.

"Does this mean I'll have a room or an extra blanket for the deck?"

Lindiwe laughed. "You will have a room, Omari Ket." She turned to Gugulethu. "Lethu, take Omari to his room. I'll finish the count."

"Yes, nahoda," the man said. He looked at Omari up and down as if inspecting a bull for sale.

"Follow me, Mikijen," he said.

Gugulethu led him into the bowels of the *Aamhle*. The ship consisted of five decks. The lowest decks were for supplies, the middle decks for stacks. The deck just below was for personnel. Omari's thoughts lingered on the crates of stacks as Gugulethu led him to his room. He'd never seen so many, not even when he was guarding the richest Kiswala nobles. He could take this ship with a team of five, sail anywhere in the world and establish his own sultanate. Omari stopped where he stood then laughed aloud. He possessed wealth much more than most Ki Khangans, and here he was planning to rob a dhow.

"Your room," Gugulethu said, gesturing at an open door.

Omari entered and was pleasantly surprised. The space contained a hammock, desk, storage chest, and a few extra compartments.

"Thank you!" he said.

"You're welcome," Gugulethu replied. "We will set sail soon. Supper will be served after we are underway."

"Can you use some help on deck?" Omari asked.

"No bwa," Gugulethu replied. "Enjoy your journey."

Gugulethu returned to his duties. Omari stored his things then climbed into the hammock. Apparently, his stacks bought more than just safe passage. This was probably one of the best cabins on the ship. His journey to Sati-Baa would be more comfortable than he anticipated. He hoped their generosity extended to the food as well.

Despite his prime treatment, Omari was restless. He went to the top deck to help like he did during his Mikijen days. The crew was suspicious for a moment until they realized he knew his way around. He labored until he was tired, then retreated to his cabin. The vessel was in open water when the evening meal was finally served. Omari enjoyed the fresh portions, knowing that such luxuries would be in short supply as their journey continued.

They were a week out when he began noticing familiar stars and coastal landmarks. After two more days, he was sure of his destination and he was not happy.

"Daarila's beard!" he cursed. He found Lindiwe at the helm, her eyes locked on the horizon.

"We're going to Kiswala!" he shouted.

Lindiwe turned to him looking annoyed. "Yes, we are."

"You're supposed to take me to Sati-Baa!"

Lindiwe sighed. "This is a working vessel. I told you that there would be dockings."

"But you didn't tell me one would be Kiswala!"

"Is that a problem, Omari?" she asked. There was a hint of suspicion in her voice. "I would think you wouldn't mind a short visit, being that you are a former Mikijen."

Omari opened his mouth to argue but then thought better of it. If he complained too much it would appear there was a serious reason he didn't want to visit, which in fact it might well be. As far as his former cohorts knew, he died in battle. If anyone he served with still lived, his reappearance might make them think he deserted, which he did. And the fact that he still possessed the ngisimaugi could cause another level of discussion.

"No, it's not a problem," he finally said. "I wasn't expecting such a long delay."

"It won't be," Lindiwe said. "You're aware of our business with the Kiswalans. They take precedence. You could use the time to visit old haunts, or you could remain on board until our business is done. That is your choice."

Omari grinned and waved his hand. "I might just do a little sightseeing," he said. "It has been some time. Ten years to be exact."

"Then you will have much to see," Lindiwe replied. "Much can change in ten years."

There was something in the way Lindiwe said those last words that put Omari on edge. He would have to get off the dhow before they arrived.

He sauntered away and small talked with the crew. When he returned to his room, he had all the information he needed. Unlike most dhows, the docking boats were stored below deck. There was no way he could carry one up without being noticed. His only other choice was to jump ship and swim to the shore. To do that he would have to wait until they were close enough. Though Omari was an excellent swimmer, he was sure someone would be waiting for him by the time he reached land, and he would be in no shape for a fight.

"Damn it to the Cleave!" he said. There was no alternative. He'd have to play this through at least until he reached landfall.

After another week on the seas the Kiswala Islands came into view. The barrier island sultanate ran along the eastern Kiswala shore, separated from the mainland by wide lagoons, marshes, and mangrove swamps. Jagged peaks rose over the ocean, some high so high their peaks were covered in ice. Omari stood at the prow as the dhow approached Kariba Harbor, surprised at the emotions he felt. He never thought he would miss the islands but as they sailed closer, he realized he did.

He heard footsteps and turned to see Lindiwe with a rare smile on her face.

"I see you're happy," Omari said.

"Happy to have you off my dhow," Lindiwe replied.

"It hasn't been that bad, has it?"

Lindiwe shrugged. "You've been a decent deck hand, and you've stayed out of my way."

Omari grinned. "I would have been happy to get in your way."

Lindiwe's smile faded. "Goodbye, Omari Ket."

She turned and began walking away then stopped. "By the way, whatever happens once we reach the shore is just business."

Omari's jaw tensed. There would be trouble. He scanned the area and the deck again for some way out, but there was none. "Damn it to the Cleave!" he said as he took his swords out then oiled them.

A few lengths from the dock Omari realized his preparation was useless. Ten Mikijen waited, their eyes on the *Aamhle*. Even at his best he wouldn't be able to fight his way through so many. His only hope was that they didn't intend to kill him.

No sooner had the dhow moored did the Mikijen board. Omari forced a smile to his face as his hands found his sword and dagger hilts. The mercenaries' grim faces transformed into friendly smiles. One of them, a tall man with ebony skin and yellow smile approached. He extended his hand, and Omari grasped his forearm as they shook.

"Welcome, brother," the man said. "I'm Areng Dak. We have been sent to escort you to the sultan's palace."

"What a minute," Omari said. "You're taking me to the palace? For what?"

"You are to be the sultan's honored guest," Areng answered.

Omari took another look around the boat and the docks, hoping for a last minute chance to escape before his shoulders slumped. Areng laughed.

"The sultan said you would look for a way to flee. He knows you very well. I assure you this is not what you think."

"The sultan knows me? Who is he?"

"That I cannot tell you," Areng replied. "You must see for yourself."

Areng walked away, waving for Omari to follow. He looked about; the baharia, Lindiwe, and Gugulethu, watched as he left the dhow.

"Alright, show's over!" Lindiwe shouted. "Let's get these goods to market!"

Areng walked beside Omari as the others cleared their way. They reached the brick street where horses waited for them. There was an extra horse for Omari. Areng paid the dock workers who watched the beasts while they were gone. They mounted and they were on their way.

Omari took in the city as he racked his brain trying to remember any Kiswala merchants that knew him. He was of no special rank when he served; in truth he was constantly reprimanded for his behavior. Omari suspected that the only reason they didn't kick him out was that he was a good fighter, and those were in short supply. All the time he continued to look about for a way out. If he could find at least one clear alleyway or street, he'd be on his way as fast as possible.

The palace came into view minutes later. Although the merchant owners lived in well-appointed homes near the docks, Kiswalans with deep bloodlines lived among the hills on the other side of the lagoon separating the mainland from the ocean. The sultan's palace rested on the crown of the highest hill, a place easily seen and easily defended. When they reached the base of the hill, they switched from horses to the mountain goats bred millennia ago for the sole purpose of scaling the high ground. Though riding the goats was not nearly as comfortable as the horses, the unusual mounts proved their worth transversing the steep, narrow roadway. Another contingent of Mikijen waited for them at the hillcrest before the sultan's palace. The massive white structure stood another hundred yards away, a crown jewel set before the jagged mainland peaks. Although the hill guards were friendly, the large number of them put Omari on edge. Things were not as calm as Areng wanted him to believe.

They dismounted and walked the remaining distance to the palace. As they reached the stairs leading into the structure, the sultan burst through the gilded palace doors followed by two heavily armed guards. A finely woven yellow silk turban rested on his head, a large emerald broach pinned in the center. A matching kanzu covered his body and brushed his sandaled feet. A bright, multi-colored khanga circled his waist, holding a jeweled jambiya. The sultan posed a few strides from Omari and grinned. Omari studied his face for a moment before recognizing him.

"Malamin? Is that you?"

Malamin Cissé approached, wrapping his arms around Omari and squeezed him tight.

"My brother! It's been so long!"

Omari returned the hug in suspicion. Although he and Malamin knew each other, they were not the type of friends that warranted the special attention Omari was receiving.

"A long time indeed," Omari said.

"I told everyone you weren't dead," Malamin replied. "Zeru was a massacre, but if anyone would come out alive it was you."

"Some of us were lucky," Omari said.

Malamin's eyes narrowed. "No, my brother, suspect it was more than luck. You were the only survivor."

Omari saw what Malamin was doing. Suggesting desertion among the Mikijen was a death sentence. That was his leverage. But he was still confused. How did Malamin become a Mikijen sultan? And how did he know Omari was alive? Omari decided to speak plainly. He had nothing to lose.

"How did you find me, why are you sultan, and why I'm here?"

"I'll answer your questions while we walk, my brother."

They ambled toward the palace flanked by the interior guards. The others returned to their duties.

"Ki Khanga is big, but rumors travel like greywings with the wind," Malamin said. "The Kiswala know that behind every rumor is a morsel of truth, so when I began hearing talk of a rogue Mikijen, I paid attention. The Kiswala didn't care. They were only concerned with information that would lead to profit. It was when I heard this mercenary still possessed the ngisimaugi that I became intrigued. The final piece arrived one day with a traveling acrobatic troupe. There was a woman whose voice was like Eda's breath who sang about her many lovers. One, she said, was as handsome as a djinn and skilled with both his swords, one of steel and the other flesh. That was when I knew it was you."

Omari smiled. There were worse ways of being remembered.

"So what?" Omari said. "You brought me back here to bed me?"

Malamin laughed. "You should be so lucky."

"Again, why am I here?"

"I thought you'd be more curious about why I'm sultan."

"I am, actually."

Malamin adjusted his robes as they entered the palace. Omari had never been inside one of the massive buildings and expected to be awed. He was. The amount of wealth on display in the entrance atrium was enough to make a poor person faint. Intricate tapestries from throughout Ki Khanga covered the towering walls, climbing to the roof painted to resemble the sky. Points of light spread across the canopy, carved openings of clear glass. He took in the scenery as Malamin spoke.

"We Mikijen were castigated by the Kiswala after Zeru. Of course they didn't care about the loss of life, only of merchandise. The tension between the Kiswala and our leaders had been building for decades, but this was the incident that cleaved the ground. A secret meeting was held that night, and we decided to revolt."

"I wouldn't call that a revolt," Omari said. "If all the Mikijen decided to move against the Kiswala there would be no one to stop them."

"If only it had been that simple," Malamin replied. "There were those among us that had no intention of defying the Kiswala. They couldn't wait to tell their masters of our plans. Later that night, they attacked our barracks. We lost many Mikijen, but not enough. We killed the traitors then went after the Kiswala."

"Daarila's beard!" Omari said. "You killed them all?"

"Not all, but enough," Malamin replied. "We needed to know where they kept their wealth, their trading logs, everything they used to run the sultanate. We also conscripted many into the ranks, preparing for their enemies to try to take advantage of the turmoil."

"Aux," Omari said. Malamin nodded. "Did they?"

Malamin shook his head. "Most of them were glad to be rid of them. Those who were allies didn't care, as long as goods continued to flow. And here we are."

Omari nodded. He knew the situation had not been as simple as Malamin described, but he didn't care for details. His main concern was why he was here.

"And that leaves me," Omari said.

"Leave us," Malamin said to his guards.

The guards bowed then left the atrium. Malamin waited until they had disappeared before speaking.

"Our rule has been volatile," Malamin said. "In the ten years since we took over, there has been eight sultans. I am the ninth. Whenever a Mikijen commander gathers enough warriors around them, they try for the throne. So far, my rule has been the longest because I've done my best to placate anyone grumbling for power. Still, there are those who plot."

Malamin placed his hand on Omari's shoulder. "Loyalty is hard to find these days. It's like a mouse hiding among the reeds. But you have been gone all these years, and you owe no one your loyalty or your sword."

"I'm a mercenary," Omari replied. "Loyalty is not a concern of mine. My sword has a price but I'm not interested in your situation. I just want to go to Sati-Baa and you're in the way. But I have a feeling that won't happen until I do what you wish. So what do I need to do to be on my way?"

"I need you to kill someone," Malamin said. "I'm willing to pay handsomely for it."

Omari had no need for stacks, but a few more wouldn't hurt. Of all the things he'd done for pay, assassination was the most distasteful. But he knew Malamin was holding one card in his hand if he refused, and he had to keep him from playing it.

"How much?" he asked.

"Forty stacks," Malamin answered.

"Cleave!" Even for someone with his wealth, forty stacks was a large amount. "This must be a dangerous person."

"She hasn't made a move yet, but my spies tell me she will. They think she conspires with the Kashites, and they're sure she wants me and the other powerful Mikijen dead all at the same time. I must strike before she does."

"How much time do I have?" Omari asked.

"How much do you need?"

"A week at least. It's been a long time since I've been here and I need time to reacquaint myself. I'll also need a map of her dwellings and grounds, and a list of necessary equipment."

Malamin frowned. "What other equipment do you need? You have a sword, strength, and your protection. I don't see what else . . ."

"Either meet my requests or find someone else," Omari said.

Malamin's face took on a dark countenance. "You must not realize the game you now play. I can walk out of this room right now and tell my guards who you are and what really happened at Zeru."

Omari grinned. He wanted to at least get that admission out of him before agreeing. He didn't have a choice. "I'll need everything in two days. I'll need the map immediately."

Malamin smiled. "Granted. Do you need any of my guards to go with you?"

"No," Omari replied. "I do such things like this alone."

"So be it," Malamin said. "But this is a daunting task. Surely, you'll need assistance."

"I don't, Omari replied. "All I need is payment when I return and freedom to leave Kiswala once it's done."

"You can leave whenever you like," Malamin said.

"Yeah. Rolled into a carpet and left out on the street."

Malamin feigned shock. "I'm surprised you don't trust me."

"Payment and safe passage," Omar replied.

"Agreed," Malamin said.

"I need a place to stay until I'm ready," Omari said.

"You will stay in the palace," Malamin replied.

"No, I won't," Omari said. "I'll get a room at a tavern by the docks. A very good room."

"As you wish," Malamin said.

"And I want half my stacks now."

Malamin scowled. "No. You'll try to run as soon as you're out of my sight."

Omari tilted his head. "And when will that be? When I'm taking a shit? Your guards and spies will be watching me every minute until I do my job or die trying."

"I see your years of wandering have seasoned you," Malamin replied. "Are you still the Omari Ket I once knew?"

"Probably not," Omari said. "But you have me by the balls. So, give me my stacks and let me get about business."

Malamin clapped his hands and the guards returned, one of them carrying a satchel of stacks. The sultan had anticipated Omari's request to his satisfaction. He exited the palace with the guards and they rode the irritable goats down to the base of the hill. Omari was happy to ride a docile horse back to the docks, where the guards took him to a small, but well-built building. They entered with him as well, walking up to an elderly woman cleaning gourds behind a bar, her grey hair hidden by a colorful head scarf. She frowned at the guards.

"What is it this time?" she said with a scowl.

"We come in peace, aunt," one of the guards said. "This man is under the patronage of the Sultan. All his expenses will be paid by the palace."

The guard took out a leather bag then placed it on the counter. The woman picked it up and opened it. A wide smile split her face when she turned her attention to Omari.

"He is our honored guest," she said.

"Thank you, aunt." The guards left the tavern, glancing at Omari on the way out. The proprietor hurried from behind the counter to Omari. She glanced at the stack bag he held.

"Welcome!" she said. "I am Afia, owner of this establishment."

"Omari."

"Well, Omari, I hope you are hungry because I'm preparing a feast just for you!"

Omari waved his hand. "No need for that. A bowl of fish stew will suffice. I'd be grateful if you'd show me my room."

"Of course! Follow me!"

Omari stood to follow Afia to the stairs leading to the rooms. As he walked, he noticed two familiar faces sitting at a corner table: Lindiwe and Gugulethu. He nodded at them and they nodded back.

The room was modestly sized with a small but comfortable looking bed, a nightstand with a used candle and storage chest at the foot of the bed. It wasn't a luxury, but it was better than a dhow cabin.

"I will bring your stew immediately," Afia said.

"Thank you."

Omari waited until Afia was gone before opening the satchel. There was something else inside it, a piece of parchment neatly folded. Omari took it out and opened it. It was a map of Kiswala, hundreds of islands dotting Ki Khanga's eastern coast. Many of them were uninhabited, homes of abundant wildlife and the occasional person seeking isolation. A star indicated the inhabited isles, with the name of each sultan written above it. One island, Pimba, was circled. Omari assumed this was where his target waited.

A knock on his door interrupted his thoughts.

"Come in," he said.

The door opened and Lindiwe entered with his stew. She sat the stew on the nightstand.

"Where's Gugulethu?" Omari asked.

"He's gone back to the dhow," she said.

"So why are you here?"

Lindiwe grinned. "Why do you think?"

Omari folded the map and put it back into the satchel.

"I thought you wanted nothing to do with me," he said. "You made that clear on your dhow."

Lindiwe sat on the bed. "I wanted nothing to do with you on my dhow. I have a reputation to maintain. But here?" She reached into her shirt then took out a bottle of palm wine.

"You should have started with the wine," he said. "But wait. I don't want my stew to get cold."

"Believe me, when we're done you won't care."

*　*　*

Omari awoke to muted sunlight. He untangled himself from Lindiwe then sat on the edge of his bed. His stomach growled and his eyes fell on the stew bowl atop his nightstand. Omari grabbed the bowl and began eating it. It was cold but satisfying.

"Leave me some," Lindiwe said.

Omari grunted as he finished it. "I'll go downstairs and get you something fresh. You earned it."

"I told you," Lindiwe replied. She stretched then yawned. "It's too early for fish stew. Ask them if they have eggs and bread."

Omari put on his clothes and went downstairs. Afia was at the bar, overseeing the scant customers. She smiled when she saw Omari.

"I take it you had a pleasant night?" she asked.

Omari smirked. "Do you have eggs and bread?"

"I do!" Afia replied.

"Can you have someone deliver it to my room when it's ready?"

"I can."

"And I'd like a beer gourd. I'll have it here."

Afia nodded then set about her tasks. Omari found an empty table far from the other patrons then took out the map and spread it atop the nicked wooden surface. It would take a day to sail to Pimba. He'd have to find a jahazi or mtepe willing to take on an extra passenger or hand. Pimba would be a difficult place to be discreet as well. It was the smallest of the Kiswala islands and the most fortified. Omari remembered the stories of its sultan being very rich and very paranoid. Omari suspected the new sultan chose the island for the same reasons.

"Your beer."

Omari looked up into the eyes of a scruffy boy holding his beer gourd between his small hands. Omari took it and the boy went about his way. He took a sip and smiled. Kiswala beer was the best in Ki Khanga, a heavy brew spiced with aromatics from lands most Ki Khangans didn't know existed. He was about to return to the map when he heard footfalls on the stairs. Lindiwe appeared, a smile on her face as she sauntered to the table and sat.

"Thank you for the breakfast," she said.

"It was the least I could do after last night," Omari replied.

Lindiwe chuckled. She looked at the map. "Planning a safari? I guess the sultan is done with you."

"I wish," Omari replied. "I'm in his employ for the moment."

"Where are you going?"

"Pimba."

Lindiwe's face scrunched up. "I don't envy you. That place is a prison. The dock guards inspect every crack and crevice before allowing you to dock. I feel violated when I leave."

"I was afraid of that," Omari replied. "I bet you have a few places to make discreet landings."

Lindiwe picked up his beer and took a sip. "I have a schedule to keep. No time for detours."

"Malamin paid me forty stacks for this job," Omari said. "Half of it is yours if you'll take me to Pimba and wait for me."

Lindiwe did a poor job hiding her surprise. Omari took his beer and finished it.

"Do we have a deal?" he asked.

"Consider my dhow at your service," Lindiwe answered. "I'll even throw in two of my mabaharia just in case you need assistance."

"I'm fine by myself," Omari said.

"You might be able to get on shore, but you don't know your way around," Lindiwe said.

"I have maps," Omari replied.

"Fuck the maps," Lindiwe said. "One of my crew is from Pimba. He's a better guide than any map."

Omari scratched his chin. "That's true. He can get me where I need to be. The rest I'll do on my own." He rolled up the map. "I guess we should be on our way."

"I was hoping we could go back upstairs," Lindiwe said.

"We'll have plenty of time on your dhow," Omari replied.

"No," Lindiwe said. "Once we're back on my dhow, I don't know you. I'll have you thrown overboard if you show otherwise."

"Well in that case," Omari said with a grin. "I'll meet you upstairs."

* * *

Omari arrived at the dock midday, an hour after Lindiwe. The crew prepared for departure, making a final inspection. As Omari approached, Gugulethu hurried down the plank, a grimace on his hard face.

"This is your doing!" he shouted.

33

Omari walked past the irate man. "I paid your nahoda to take me to my destination. If you have any quarrel, it's with her."

"You know what I'm talking about," Gugulethu shouted. "She wouldn't be doing this if you hadn't . . ."

"If he hadn't what, Lethu?"

Lindiwe stood on deck, her arms folded across her chest. She barely noticed Omari as he boarded.

Gugulethu confronted Lindiwe. "How could you let him do this? We have obligations to other clients that are more important!"

"Last time I checked, this was my dhow," Lindiwe replied. "I decide what we do and when we do it. Our clients are important but not vital. They will wait; they have no choice. If we lose one or two, they can be replaced."

"This is not good business," Gugulethu said. "We can't be seen as lax just because some rogue mercenary made you . . ."

"This discussion is over," Lindiwe said. "Go be about your business, Lethu."

Gugulethu's eyes narrowed and he marched away.

"It seems your first mate is serious about your schedule," Omari said.

"This has nothing to do with our schedule," Lindiwe replied.

Omari grinned. "I see. I'll go to my room. It's the same one, right?"

"Yes," Lindiwe replied.

Omari found his cabin and unpacked his belongings. He sat at the desk and took out a second parchment, a detailed drawing of the Pimba sultan's palace. Like the island, the ruler's residence was smaller than other Kiswala strongholds. The sultan's room was on the second floor overlooking the city. There was one window; whether it was big enough for him to enter he wouldn't know until he saw it himself. He set the palace map aside and took out the island drawing. He was studying the streets when his door opened and Lindiwe entered and glanced at the map. Omari grinned.

"So you changed your mind?"

34

"No. I need you on deck," she replied. "You'll be working your way to Pimba."

"Aren't I a guest?"

"You were, until Gugulethu quit," Lindiwe said. "I need the extra hand."

She left his room. Omari rolled up the map then stripped down to his breeches. He would look at the maps later. For now, there was work to do.

* * *

From a distance, Pimba seemed like a smooth solid piece of rock jutting from the sea. Upon closer inspection, the irregularities of surface revealed themselves. Small homes built from island stone scaled the surface with small patches of arable land. Somewhere along the narrow streets, undulating hills, and tight neighborhoods was the sultan's palace, Omari's objective.

Omari stood on the deck, smoking his chagga pipe. A baharia strummed a small ngoni, his singing and playing just good enough to be entertaining. If all went well, he'd soon be on his way to Sati-Baa, with nothing to worry about behind him.

"You have any more of that?"

Lindiwe walked beside him then gazed into the horizon.

"If you're willing to share," Omari replied.

Lindiwe held out her hand and Omari handed her the pipe. Lindiwe took a long drag then handed it back to him. Omari watched as she exhaled the smoke from her nostrils.

"Good leaf," she said.

"Only the best," Omari replied. "I thought we weren't to acknowledge each other on your dhow."

"I'm only sharing a smoke with a fellow baharia," she said.

"You sure that's all?" Omari asked.

"Yes," Lindiwe answered.

Omari shrugged then turned his attention back to Pimba.

"What is it you're going to do once you reach Pimba?" Lindiwe asked.

"Kill the sultan," Omari replied.

Lindiwe laughed until she realized Omari wasn't.

"You're serious?"

Omari nodded. Lindiwe scowled as she stepped away from him.

"Why did you involve me in this?'

"I didn't. I asked you to take me to Pimba and return me to the mainland. That's all."

"The Cleave you didn't!" Lindiwe said. "If you had told me why I would have refused. If you fail, I'll be implicated!"

"First of all, you didn't ask. I would have. Second, I won't fail," Omari replied.

"Once you're off my dhow, I don't want to see you again!"

"Then give me my stacks back."

Lindiwe's mouth shrank. "What?"

"Give me my stacks back," Omari repeated. "I paid for my journey here and back. If you're not going to bring me back, you don't deserve to be paid. And don't try to keep them. You know who I am, and what I'm capable of."

Lindiwe swept her hand across the deck. "My crew would be very disappointed if they discovered they weren't being paid."

Omari glanced around. "I'm sure they would be. But your crew are not fighters. You maybe, but the rest? No. You would be the first person I'd killed. So the others would have to decide who would be alive to collect their pay and how they would collect it with me dead."

"Daarila's Beard!" Lindiwe said. "I'll take you and bring you back. That's all. That's it."

"Excellent. Now that that's settled . . ."

"You're out of your mind!"

Lindiwe stomped way. Omari watched her until she went below deck before laughing. He was surprised his bluff worked. He'd sooner jump ship than fight the entire crew. This plan was getting more convoluted with every second. The sooner it was done, the better.

The island was close enough for all its details to be revealed. The navigator steered the dhow away from the main port long before it was visible from the shore, working the vessel to the opposite side of the island. Omari was on deck with all his gear, looking about for the person Lindiwe insisted he take with him. The nahoda appeared a few minutes later with a man almost as tall as Omari and half his girth. Omari recognized him as the baharia who climbed the masts and kept the sails in good condition. He was older but didn't lack in strength or endurance.

"Omari, this is Mosi. He will be your guide."

Omari shook his hand. Mosi's grip was firm and sure.

"Where to you wish to go?" Mosi asked.

"The sultan's palace," Omari replied.

Mosi rubbed his cheek. "I can get you there, but I can't get you in, if that's what you're trying to do."

"Why would you think that?" Omari asked.

"Because you have the look of a thief about you," Mosi replied.

Omari couldn't deny Mosi's opinion of him because the man was right. He gave him a pat on the shoulder. "I like you. I do need to get in. All you have to do is get me there."

Mosi nodded. Lindiwe looked into the distance. "We're here."

Omari turned his attention to the island. A sheer stone cliff rose over the ocean waters.

"We're supposed to climb that?"

Mosi laughed. "It looks impossible from a distance, which is why no one ever stops. But there's a way up the cliffs. It's also a faster way to the palace. I'll show you."

"Your maps would have never told you that," Lindiwe said.

"Let's be off then," Omari replied. "The sooner we get there, the sooner we get back."

"Good luck, Mosi," Lindiwe said. She had no words for Omari. He shook his head then followed Mosi to the stern where a small boat waited. They climbed in, then two baharia lowered them onto the calm ocean surface.

Mosi and Omari made good time to the shore. The sheer cliffs revealed their irregularity as they neared. There was a narrow strip of land at the base of the cliffs, a grainy black beach spotted with large boulders. Mosi stopped rowing then pointed to the right.

"That's our way up," he said.

Omari saw the cave. Water flowed out the entrance, the fresh liquid mingling with the salty sea. They rowed in its direction, beaching the boat a few lengths away.

"Are we swimming up the stream?" Omari asked.

"No," Mosi replied. "There is a trail that runs along the right bank. It gets narrow in places but otherwise it's safe. Unless we run into someone."

"Why should that happen?"

"The stream runs through the palace," Mosi replied. "The stories say that it's been used as an escape route more than once."

Omari could imagine some sultan stumbling down the stream side, attempting to hold up their kanga and their dignity. He laughed.

"What's so funny?" Mosi asked.

"Nothing. Let's get to it."

Then took out the torches they brought with them then lit them. Mosi led the way, Omari staying close behind. It took them an hour to traverse the cave to the surface. When they entered the dense forest outside the cavern it was still night. Omari plopped on his haunches as soon as they exited the cave, tired and wet from the steep climb. Mosi stood over hm, disappointment on his narrow face.

"Get up," he said. "We have a long way to go."

Omari dusted off his clothes then stood.

"Lead the way, task master."

The trail became a road as it neared the palace. Other travelers joined Omari and Mosi, none seemingly interested in them. Omari studied the royal building's exterior, referencing it to what he remembered from his map. They passed the window leading to the sultan's room and it took everything in his power not to stop and stare. At a glance it looked like a height he could scale without a rope, but he would secure one just in case. He moved close to Mosi.

"This is it," he said. "I'll need a rope and grappling hooks."

"I know where you can get them," Mosi replied. "Follow me."

They continued until they reached the main city. It resembled most others of Kiswala, with the exception of kamba statues occupying every intersection. The round flat crustaceans were brightly colored; their claws raised over their bodies as if in supplication.

"Why all the kamba statues?" Omari said.

"It's a local deity," Mosi quickly replied. "Kahabu."

"Are they this large?" Omari asked.

"I've only seen small ones," Mosi replied. "Some say there are giants in the depths of the sea, some the size of a dhow."

Omari nodded. His experience told him to be wary. He'd encountered many creatures and humans said not to exist, and many were more terrible than the stories that made them legends.

They walked the streets of the island city, being careful to avoid the constables. A look of despair seemed to be etched into the faces of everyone. Not one person smiled, and no one made eye contact with them longer than a second.

They wandered into the market district for food. The merchants were cold and distant, taking their orders and money with a dearth of enthusiasm. Omari had never seen a place so despondent, even in the aftermath of battle.

"Something is wrong here," he finally said.

"Yes, it is," Mosi replied. "It's as if Eda has turned her back on these people."

"It's not her," Omari replied. "It's something different."

"Whatever it is, I don't like it. I'm going back to the cave once we're done."

"This is your home," Omari said.

"It doesn't feel like it," Mosi replied.

Mosi led them to the blacksmith district. The borough sang with the rhythm of hammers striking anvils, the smoke from small furnaces clouding the sky.

"That one," Omari said, pointing at a solitary smithy with no customers. The blacksmith sat on an iron stool, wearing a dingy shirt covered by a leather apron. He sipped beer from a metal gourd, probably of his own making. He acknowledged them with a head nod as they approached.

"Greetings," he said with a raspy voice. "I am Rubani Waweru. How can I help you?"

"We need grappling hooks," Mosi said.

The smithy raised an eyebrow. "Not a common request."

"Do you have them?" Omari asked.

Rubani stood then walked into his workshop. He bypassed his anvil and forge, leading them to the back of the building. He went to a crate covered by an oiled blanket then pulled it back. Rubani hunted through the crate then pulled out a pair of thick grappling hooks.

"These look strong enough to hold a man's weight," he said with a smirk. "I assume you'll need rope, too?"

Omari grinned. "Yes."

"I have that, too."

They followed Rubani to another container with woven leather rope. He rolled out a length then handed it to Omari.

"How much?" Omari asked.

"Ten cowries."

"Ten cowries!" Mosi exclaimed. "That's ridiculous!"

Omari took ten cowries out of his pouch and paid the smithy. "Eda bless."

The smithy smiled as he took the cowries. "Eda bless. Don't get caught."

The smithy gave them a leather bag for their purchase and they were on their way. They stopped in the market for dried fish and bread then retired to the outskirts of the town near the bush. They ate in silence, still disturbed by the behavior of the Pimba inhabitants.

"Why are you doing this?" Mori finally asked. "Lindiwe will take you anywhere you want to go for what you paid her. You can go on to Sati-Baa and no one here would be the wiser."

"I wish it was that easy," Omari replied. "I don't like loose ends, and I don't need anyone hunting me down for their money. Plus, I gave your nahoda all my advance. I don't get the rest until I return with proof that Pimba's sultan is dead."

Mori shook his head then finished his meal. "I'm going back to the cave. You remember the way, don't you?"

"Yes."

"Good. Make sure no one follows you. I'd hate to lose a good secret path."

"It depends on how I'm leaving," Omari said.

40

Mori frowned. "Goodbye, Omari. I hope I see you again, but I doubt it."

Mori disappeared into the bush before Omari could insult him. He finished his food then went back to the town. Omari didn't want to spend the rest of the day hiding, especially if it might be his last. He found a serving house near the main market and attempted to interest some of the locals in a game of oware, but they said no. Omari thought it might be because they saw him as a stranger, but he'd experienced such treatment before, and this wasn't it. The establishment was silent except for the sounds of utensils clattering against plates and the chewing of food. Conversations were sparse, and laughter nonexistent. These people were joyless. It was as if life was something to endure, not enjoy. He thought about Mori's words, about walking away and taking the chance that he wouldn't be pursued but shook his head. He would do this.

Night finally fell across the town and Omari set about on his task. The sun was well below the horizon, and the sliver of moonlight replacing it did little to illuminate the night sky. Despite the darkness Omari kept to the corners and alleyways, making sure to avoid the night constables, of which there were many.

He expected security to increase as he neared the citadel, but what he experienced was just the opposite. A few strides from the palace the streets were completely empty. The only people about were the guards protecting the compound walls, and they were scarce. Omari's stomach tightened; this was a bad sign. If the sultan needed no physical protection, other forces were at work. How far was he willing to go to fulfill his obligations? Once again, the urge to abandon the entire deal surfaced, yet descended just as quickly. He didn't need Mikijen hunting him; he knew how persistent they could be. But there was something not setting right with him and about this mission. He decided to compromise. He would enter the palace, but he would not do any harm. Pimba's sultana would not die, but she would no longer sit upon the stool. Changa decided he would kidnap her then set her free once she was far enough away not to cause any problems. The Kashites would no doubt pay dearly for her, but even Omari would not take a person to a place that would be worse than death.

"Daarila's balls!" he said.

Omari finally returned to the spot he and Mosi selected as the best entry. He scanned the area before taking the grappling hooks and rope from the bag. He hid his swords in the bush, taking only his daggers. Omari didn't expect to encounter any resistance and if he did, he was more than capable in handling it with his small blades.

Omari tied the hooks to the rope. He spun the hooks for momentum then threw them toward the open window. His old skills from the Sati-Baa streets didn't fail him; the hook sailed through the window. He waited for a few moments, making sure the hook had not been seen before jerking the rope. The hooks bit into the ledge; Omari pulled with his full body weight to make sure it was secure before beginning his climb.

Although his hook throwing skills were intact, his climbing skills weren't. Omari tumbled through the window out of breath. He sat on the stone floor gathering himself as he studied his situation. A long hall extended before him, lit with small torches mounted at regular intervals. According to his map, the sultan's room was at the end of the corridor.

Omari crept down the hall. Each torch was mounted by a room entrance. He peered inside each and was impressed. They were storage rooms, holding the sultan's wealth. One room was filled with spice urns; another with rare fabrics from throughout Ki Khanga. There was a room containing rare jewels, another with precious metals. Omari's anxiety increased with each room passed. This palace held amazing wealth; where were the guards?

He reached the sultan's lair. Torches burned on both sides of the closed doors. The jeweled portal was a hand carved Kiswala masterpiece, the edges accented with cowry shells. Omari placed his palm against the aged wood then pushed. The door moved and he snatched it way.

"Don't do it," Omari whispered. But he had to.

Omari continued and the door creaked open. Standing on the far side of the room was Sultana Hasnaa, a tall, regal woman dressed in a sheer night dress before an elaborate bed.

The lines creasing her forehead and at the corners of her mouth hinted at her age. She stared at him calmly, as if she expected him. Omari entered the room, his knives drawn. So this is who he was sent to kill. The sultan showed no fear. It was as if she was waiting for him.

"Should I call my guards?" the sultana asked.

"Only if you don't like them," Omari replied.

"Who sent you?" she asked.

"Doesn't it matter?"

Hasnaa sighed. "I guess it doesn't. How much are they paying you?"

Omari stopped. "Forty stacks."

"I'll pay you eighty."

Omari's eyes went wide.

"Why do you hesitate?" Hasnaa asked. "I'm sure you're not struggling with your conscience. You left your loyalty to the Mikijen long ago, Omari Ket." Hasnaa smiled. "Yes, I know who you are."

"And what do you want in return?" Omari asked.

"I want you to go away and never return to Kiswala."

Omari lowered his knives. "Guarantee me safe passage from Kiswala and you have a deal."

Hasnaa smiled. "Done. Follow me."

The woman walked by Omari into the corridor. She took one of her bedroom door torches from its bracket and continued. Omari followed, his senses high. Dealing with those that only valued money was a dangerous thing, with treachery around every corner if the price was right. He could end this, killing the woman and taking whatever Malamin had offered. But the chance to collect more stacks was too tantalizing. He grinned at the absurdity of it all; he was already rich beyond his imagination, yet he followed a person that offered a bit more. The perfect definition of greed. At least he could say wealth hadn't changed him.

Hasnaa led him down another dimly lit corridor. She opened a door and they entered another dark room.

"Stay here," Hasnaa said. She walked along the wall, her torchlight revealing shelves of stacks. She stopped before a leather satchel and took it from its resting place. Omari was impressed. Eighty stacks were a hefty sum and weight and she handled it with ease. She ambled to Omari then dropped the bag at his feet.

"You can count it if you like."

Omari grinned. "No need to. It sounds right."

The woman smiled. "It was a pleasure doing business with you, Omari Ket. May Kwelikaa accept my offering with gratitude."

Omari looked confused. "What?"

There was a bright flash of pain, then nothing.

* * *

Omari awoke naked on a cold stone floor with a nasty bump on his head. He groaned as he sat up, reaching to touch his wound but thought better of it. His ngisimaugi warmed with his consciousness, slowing healing the injury.

Torches flared a few strides from where he lay, revealing a circular room. Standing against the wall were people of various sizes, upper bodies bare. Each wore blue loincloths and grotesque masks covering their faces.

"Hai Haa!" someone shouted.

Drumming filled the room, a slow, steady rhythm which implied pending doom. Omari had observed many rituals across many lands and he knew whatever was about to happen would not be good for him. The Hasnaa's words came back to him, the ones he heard before he was ambushed.

"May Kwelikaa accept my offering with gratitude."

"Shit," he whispered.

Hasnaa entered the circle, careful to stay behind the masked acolytes. She was dressed the same as the others with the exception of a long cloak hanging from her shoulders. She smiled at Omari, and he answered with a scowl.

"Omari Ket, Mikijen deserter," she said. "Did you think you could disgrace our order and never pay the consequences? Of course you did. From what I know of you, you were never a deep thinker. What else could one expect from Sati-Baa street scum?"

Omari stood. "Save your insults. I've been called worse than anything your small brain could conjure. What do I owe the Mikijen? It was either that or a death sentence. I'm sure your reason for becoming one was just as foul."

Anger twisted the woman's face. "It doesn't matter how we came to be. What matters is our oath, not to the Kiswala, but to each other. You broke that oath!"

Omari shrugged. "Oaths are always broken. Promises are never kept. That's what I learned as street scum."

"I'm happy you feel this way," Hasnaa said. "It makes it more satisfying to do this."

"Enjoy your brief reprieve," Omari said. "Malamin will send someone else."

The woman grinned. "Malamin and I serve the same master. Everything he told you was to get you here. There are others that would see you dead, those much higher than us."

Those words puzzled Omari for a moment. He was only a mercenary, a man making his way the best he could. What would powerful people want with him?

Hasnaa turned and walked away, followed by the acolytes. Five Mikijen entered the chamber, swords drawn. They took defensive stances but did not advance. The were not there to kill him, just to keep him from trying to get out. Omari relaxed, his hand on his hips. There was no way out of this. His time had come. He looked around, hoping to see some sign or image from Eda, but there was none. There were no more options.

"Daarila, I will see you soon," he said.

Omari attacked the guards. They laughed as he ran at them, his bare feet slapping the concrete, his manhood swinging back and forth. Together they raised their swords.

"Don't kill him!" Hasnaa's voice reverberated off the chamber walls. "Kwelikaa prefers its meal alive."

The guards ignored her and attacked. Omari left himself open to the first guard's attack then quickly ducked his swing before driving his fist into the man's gut. The guard doubled over while Omari snatched the sword from his weak grip. At least now he had a sword.

Omari deflected the second guard's sword swing for his neck, the blade cutting his shoulder. He shifted, blocking the swing of the third. A Mikijen could only be confirmed dead if they were decapitated, such was the healing powers of the ngisimaugi. As he battled the remaining three guards, his suspicions were confirmed. Becoming the rulers of Kiswala made the Mikijen soft. Better warrior would have attempted to distract him before going for his neck. Ten years ago his head would already be rolling on the stones.

Their fight was interrupted by the sound of stone grating against stone. The guards turned in terror and ran. Omari followed, glancing back at the opening wall. The guards pounded against the door, but it would not open. Omari kept his eyes on the open space where the wall had been, his legs bent, sword in hand. A clacking sound rose over the cries and pleas of the guards and the largest kamba Omari had ever seen ran into the room.

"Kwelikaa," Omari whispered.

The giant crustacean hesitated then scampered toward them. Omari pounced to the left, ready to defend himself but the beast ignored him. Instead, it attacked the guards, cutting them apart with its massive pincers then shoveled their pieces into its mouth. Omari bolted for the opening, blocking out the cries of the hapless guards while grateful to Eda for the distraction. He was almost to the portal when he heard the clacking growing louder behind him. Kwelikaa wasn't satisfied with the meal before it; it wanted more.

Omari ran faster. He was near the opening when the wall began to close. He closed his eye and dove, praying to Eda he would make the jump. He dropped onto the hard surface then drew his legs in just as the wall slammed onto Kwelikaa. The creature let out a piercing screech as its carapace cracked under the tremendous weight, green ichor spewing upward and onto Omari. He wiped his face, watching the crushed deity flailing subside until it stilled. Its body kept the wall from completely closing.

"You ignorant fools!" Hasnaa shouted. "Look what you've done!"

Omari heard the door open and the sound of sandals smacking stones. Instead of fleeing, he crawled under the suspended wall, praying to Eda that it would not collapse until he had the chance for a desperate play.

"What do we do?" one of the acolytes asked.

"Harvest the eggs," Hasnaa ordered. "They should be fertile now that she's fed. We'll send slaves to clean this up later."

"What about the sacrifice?" the other acolyte asked.

"Forget about him," Hasnaa said. "The wall either crushed or crippled him. May Daarila spit in his face."

Omari waited as Hasnaa and the acolytes cut open the massive kamba and extracted the wet egg sac from its abdomen. He lay still, watching the others leave. Luckily, they left the door open. He sprinted across the floor and down a passage which led to a staircase to the observation platform. The worshippers had fled, leaving only Hansaa and her guards. Omari attacked, decapitating the guard closest to him before he could move then drove his sword into the second guard's heart. Hasnaa moved fast to grab a fallen guard's sword, but not fast enough. Omari's blade touched the back of her neck.

"Go ahead," she said. "Once the people discover their god is dead, they'll kill us all, including you."

"Not until I get my stacks," Omari replied.

"You must be kidding!"

Omari pressed the blade against Hasnaa neck, piercing her skin and drawing blood. "I'm not."

Hasnaa swallowed hard then walked, Omari close behind. They made their way back to the treasury; the bags she tossed him were still on the floor.

"Take it," she said. "May Daarila stomp you into dust."

Omari grabbed the bags then went back toward the door.

"You're letting me live?" Hansaa said.

Omari grinned. "Why should I waste my time? With Kwelikaa dead, your people will do it for me. Or maybe they won't. Either way, I don't care."

Hansaa eyes narrowed. "Flee while you can, Omari Ket. After this night, you'll be the most hunted person in all Ki Khanga."

Her words sent a chill through Omari. He turned and ran down the hallways until he reached the window through which he arrived. He threw the stack bags out then shimmied down the rope. Picking up the bags, he bolted to the secret cave, splashing, stumbling, and swimming down until he reached the beach. He searched about until he found the signal torch and flint. After lighting the torch he waved it twice as he was told, then doused it in seawater. Omari plopped down on his naked ass, took a deep breath of relief, and waited.

A boat appeared on the waves rowed by a single man. Omari stood then waded into the water, the warm waves flowing over his feet and up to his knees. The craft rode the waves to the shallows, and Mori jumped out holding a rope. He took a good look at Omari then laughed.

"You did it!" he said.

"You bet on me, didn't you?" Omari asked.

"I betted for you and against you," Mori replied. "Let's go."

They went back to the shore for the stack bags. There was an extra oar, so together they rowed back to the ship. Mabaharia lined the bulwark when they reached the dhow. The cargo net was lowered and they climbed aboard. Lindiwe waited astern, her eyes lingering on his filthy nude form as he ambled toward her. Omari grinned, striding as if he was clothed in the finest garments. He dropped the bags at her feet.

"So you killed her?" she asked.

Omari shook his head. "I didn't have to. After what occurred, the people will save me the trouble."

"What happened?" she asked.

"Let me clean up and I'll tell you all about it . . . eventually."

Lindiwe smirked. "So it's back to Kiswala?"

"Cleave no!" Omari replied. "I have enough. No need for Malamin's pay." Omari wasn't going to tell Lindiwe the real reason he didn't want to return. If he did, she'd toss him off her dhow.

"Then where to?"

Omari grinned. "Surprise me."

Hide and Seek

Omari smelled death. He eased off the road he'd been following for days, drawing his sword as he stepped into the dense bush. He crouched among the dense shrubs as he scanned the surroundings. His seasoned senses told him there had been a recent battle nearby, and he was not one to take chances. A fortune waited for him in Sati-Baa, and he was determined to live long enough to spend it.

His instincts told him to avoid what was up ahead, but his empty stomach and parched throat overruled them. If he was lucky, he would find enough among the dead to satisfy him until he reached the next village or city. That is if the killing grounds had not already been scavenged. There was only one way to find out.

He worked his way toward the stench, keeping low and staying observant. Thatch roof huts rose over the vegetation before him; at least the village hadn't been burned down, which was a good sign. As he came closer, he became less wary. Whatever happened had occurred days ago. He was safe for now.

He emerged into the open ground between the bush and the hapless town. Whoever had done this did not come for bounty, for dead livestock and people lay together in morbid poses. Omari scowled. The victors seemed to have spared no one. He knew more than anyone how cruel war could be, but knowing did not make reality any easier to bear.

There was something else he noticed among the dead. Every deceased seemed to be of the village, wearing similar fabrics and ornaments. Either their attackers had taken their dead with them, or they had suffered no losses. The latter was impossible. Even the ineptest fighters would get lucky. There was also no sign of scavengers; no tai perched on roofs or branches, no fisi roaming the streets for a morbid meal, their unsettling laugh-like voices marring the silence. An uneasiness settled on his shoulders. He should leave, but his hunger insisted he quell it before moving on.

Omari entered a hut. Luckily, it was empty. He found a gourd half full of beer that he drank quickly. An open bag of sorghum sat nearby; if he found a gourd of water or a well, he could make a fire and cook it. He put the bag in his pouch then left the hut. As he walked to the next hut, something flashed just outside of his vision. Omari swung about with his sword but saw nothing. He was about to continue when he saw it again. This time he turned and struck out his blade. He was rewarded with the startled cry of a kunguru. The black bird barely dodged his sword, cawing as it flew toward the bush.

"Daarila's beard!" he said. "Stupid bird."

He sheathed his sword and continued his search for food and water. He discovered another bag of sorghum and a few yams. His hunt took him to the village well where he filled his extra gourd. Satisfied with his bounty, he searched for a place to set up camp. Omari had no desire to spend the night among the dead, but he also didn't relish sulking in the bush. He began walking along the main road which inclined slightly as it neared the town center. Omari picked up his pace; if he was lucky this town was wealthy enough to have a small collection of nobles whose homes would contain suitable loot and better shelter. The thought made him laugh. It was hard to shake of the ways of a desperate mercenary despite the valuable anklet on his right leg and the stack bags strapped to his back.

He was rewarded with the sight of a mudbrick wall decorated with colorful geometric designs. This was most likely the chief's compound, and the fact that it was well maintained meant there would be things to collect. Even if the town was plundered, looters always missed something. For Omari, he hoped it was something he could eat and drink.

A grisly sight took shape as he neared the wall. Mangled bodies were strewn about, the heaviest concentration blocking the entrance to the compound. Whatever had happened, its climax occurred before the compound, the warriors choosing this ground as their last stand. Their bodies blocked the compound's entrance, so Omari had no choice but to climb over them. He scowled as his feet sank into decaying flesh, but his hunger would not be denied.

The inside of the compound resembled the village, with bodies scattered about. No jewelry had been taking, and cowrie pouches remained full.

"I shouldn't be here," Omari whispered, and yet he continued walking.

He finally found what he was searching for. Inside the chief's home was a wealth of dried fruits, meats, and palm wine. Omari located a woven bag and filled it with the bounty. It was all he needed and more. He ate a handful of the fruit and washed it down with palm wine, finally quieting his ravenous hunger.

"Time to leave this graveyard," he said.

He left the compound, making the grim climb over the body mound once again. Omari trotted down the road leading from the village, relieved to be leaving such a strange and ominous scene. As he approached the town market, a stinging sensation filled his nostrils. He sniffed, which proved to be the wrong response. The stinging became a burning, clawing feeling that overcame his nasal passages, his throat, and then his lungs. It felt like the worst type of drowning, his lungs filling with mucus. Omari fell to his knees then onto his back, gagging as his breathing passages flooded. Then he felt the warmth on his back as he choked then coughed himself clear, the ngisimaugi activating to save him once again. His lungs cleared and his coughing subsided. Omari rolled onto his right side and saw the strangest creature he'd ever encountered. It resembled a ngiri; short legs, wide torso dense with stiff hairs, and an extended snout. But unlike the ngiri, there were no large tusks extending from its mouth. Instead, there were rows of smaller fangs on either side, each fang releasing a yellowish white smoke. The beast vibrated, its small eyes on Omari. A spiked collar circled its neck, an indication that it belonged to someone . . . or something.

Omari remained on the ground as his strength returned. The beast ceased trembling and the lethal smoke wafting from its blunted tusks subsided. Omari could jump to his feet and run, but curiosity filled his mind. He wanted to see what controlled the beast, and he wanted to kill them for trying to kill him. Whether he could, he didn't know.

51

A drumming sound rose from a distance. The ngiri-like beast responded with a bellow that reverberated against Omari's head. A few minutes later two armored people walked into Omari's prostrated view. Both wore masks covering their mouths and noses, leaving their intense sepia eyes exposed. They carried long spears with extremely jagged edges. From the look of the village victims, they had not used the weapons on them. Omari suspected it was the toxic fumes of the ngiri beast that caused their demise, but to create such mass carnage there had to be more than one.

"Come on, stray!" one of warriors said in a deep gruff voice. "We are done here."

The warrior reached into a pouch dangling from his belt then extracted a morsel of food. The creature squealed before eating the food from his hand.

"Wait," the other person said. She pointed at Omari with her spear. "This one is different. Look at his clothing."

The duo crept closer to Omari, their spears lowered. The beast turned toward him and began its eerie vibrating. Omari considered playing dead but had no desire to experience the beast's odiferous assault again. He sprang to his feet, drawing his sword and dagger as he attacked.

"Cleave!" the man nearest to him shouted. He tried to stab Omari with his spear but he was too slow. Omari's blade split his throat. The second warrior attacked as the first man fell, charging Omari with her spear. Omari knocked it aside with his dagger then blocked the second jab with his sword. Whoever the woman was, she was skilled with the spear, almost as good as a Mikijen. They did a dangerous dance, jabbing, slicing, and stabbing at each other until Omari trapped the spear shaft under his arm then broke the woman's nose with the hilt of his sword. She fell to the ground unconscious He was about to deal a killing blow when he heard the ngiri squeal. He broke away and ran to the dead man, grabbing his mask and securing it to his face before the swine unleashed its debilitating fumes.

Omari secured the mask just in time. A cloud spewed from the animal's maw, much heavier than the one that crippled him earlier. Omari picked up the dead warrior's spear then threw it. The spearhead pierced through the ngiri's skull then entered the ground. The beast squealed, attempting to pull itself free from the impalement before succumbing and falling limp. Omari was rushing toward the body to retrieve the spear when he heard others approaching. He sprinted toward the bush, but not fast enough. An arrow whizzed by his head, nicking his ear. Omari ducked under the thick foliage, the footfalls of his pursuers drawing closer. He ran until he reached the thickest part of the bush, then turned to fight.

He took full advantage of the cover and confusion, striking down his assailants one by one. Omari struck like a hidden viper, felling his opponents like weeds to an invisible scythe. It took them a few more minutes to realize their pursuit was futile.

"Pull back!" a gruff voice shouted.

Omari stayed still until he detected no movement. He was about to creep away until his pursuers began speaking.

"Are you sure it was him?" the gruff voice asked.

"I'm sure. I saw the mark on the back of his hand."

"So it's true. Damn it to the Cleave. Things are in motion. We must return to camp and bring back the others. He can't be allowed to escape."

Omari felt a chill despite the warm clime. They were looking for him. He began making a mental list of all those who would have a grudge against him, a list of those who would wish to do him harm and he stopped. The list was too long. But who would have the means to send such a large group after him?

He imagined hordes of warriors roaming the roads and trails of Ki Khanga, seeking to end his life. That would happen if these men managed to leave. But maybe he was exaggerating. Maybe this was the only group seeking him. The fact remained that he could end it here or spend the rest of his life running with no chance to spend the wealth waiting for him in Sati-Baa. There was only one option.

Omari rushed from his hiding place, a Mikijen yell bursting from his throat. He threw the spear into the throat of the gruff man, silencing him forever. The second man went down with Omari's dagger in his forehead. The other men attacked, angry at seeing their companions struck down so wantonly. Omari ripped the spear from the gruff man's throat and met their attack. Of all the famed warriors of Ki Khanga, none were better than a skilled Mikijen with a good spear, and this spear was better than any Omari had wielded. He was a lethal tempest, stabbing, slashing, and bludgeoning his attackers until they all lay still on the ground around him. Omari panted as he let the spear tip drop to the dirt, his minor wounds healing as he observed his brutal work. He stabbed each warrior again to make certain no one would rise and alert whomever waited. He then rummaged through their pouches, gathering whatever provisions they carried before hurrying away.

It was almost dark when Omari felt a familiar and annoying presence. He looked to his left to see Eda walking beside him, and all his dark emotions dissipated.

"Why didn't you tell me I was being hunted?" he asked. He wanted to sound angry, but instead his voice was curious.

"I needed to know how you would react," Eda replied. "I needed to know if you were still worth my attentions."

"You are Eda," Omari replied. "You could command me to do anything and I could not refuse."

"There might come a time that you will have the choice."

"I don't believe you."

Eda laughed and Omari was filled with joy.

"I'm glad you are the one," she said. "Even if you fail, the journey will have been worth it."

"I'm glad you're entertained."

"Continue your travel, Omari Ket. You will see Sati-Baa. That I assure you. But your path will be most interesting."

Omari frowned. "That's what I'm afraid of."

The Match

Dry season was upon Asanteman, and Omari tasted it in his mouth. He'd been on the road for two weeks, following a merchant train through the countryside and headed in the general direction of his destination, the Sati-Baa Sea. From there it would be an easy journey to The Shining Jewel. Omari smiled as he imagined all the wonderful things awaiting him. With the wealth around his ankle, the possibilities would be almost endless.

Omari could travel much faster alone, but after the incident with the assassins in the village, he thought it better to be among others, if only for them to provide a barrier between him and his assailants. It was also good to be among company, if only for a good game of oware and a long night of drinking, and maybe a tryst or two with a willing woman in one of the villages. Unfortunately, the last opportunity hadn't come available in quite some time. He'd spent most of the stacks he took from Kiswala, keeping just enough to get him to Sati-Baa. The real prize waited there for him to claim.

The city that filled their horizon on that particular day was much larger than most. It rested on the banks of a river that flowed from the nearby hills, its forests and fields still green despite the dry season. They strolled on a wide road bordered by rich fields of sorghum, yams, and millet interspersed with cattle and goat pens, all signs of a prosperous metropolis. Omari's eyes brightened as he observed the inhabitants; they were a robust, handsome people with brown copper skin, full lips, and faces enhanced with scarification and tattoos. Omari noticed groups of women looking at him then murmuring among themselves before bursting out in laughter. A few gave him long stares, smirking when he smiled and nodded. He took note, studying their faces and clothing so he'd recognize them if he encountered them later.

The traders finally reached the merchant depot. A group of stable hands approached Kofi Donkor, the burly Asanteman trail master. The man wore a bright kenté outfit, its blue based pattern signifying his family and his guild. He greeted the stable master in the local language, and after a heated conversation and exchange of payment, the two men grasped each other's shoulders in agreement. The stable master waved to his workers and they took charge of the beasts.

Kofi approached Omari with wide arms and a brilliant smile. He wrapped Omari in one of his infamous hugs and Omari hugged him in return.

"Eda blessed me with your protection, Mikijen Man," Kofi said.

"A random circumstance," Omari corrected. He was certain Eda had nothing to do with their encounter. She would have told him of any fateful meetings, and this did not warrant her attention.

"There is no such thing as random," Kofi replied. "But let's talk of other things. Farakunda has an excellent tavern. We can drink all night, trade lies, and if we're lucky, a woman will take us to bed and put us to sleep properly."

"Lead the way," Omari replied.

Most of the laborers turned down Kofi's offer for a good meal and entertainment, opting to take their rest with the town laborers. Farakunda was home for some of them, and they were anxious to see family after such a long journey. Omari was not one to turn down a free meal, especially from the man who held the cowries.

The tavern, called The Akoben, sat just outside the merchant district, the perfect location for weary travelers. The modest building possessed a hostel above the drinking and dining area. The patrons shared a friendly greeting with Kofi; their welcome for Omari was more subdued, which was understandable. They did not know him, and as Kofi's bodyguard they might find themselves staring at the business end of his sword. As they sat, a tall woman wearing a flowing dress and dozens of necklaces sauntered to the table, her jewels playing a discordant song. Her hazel eyes lingered on Omari before focusing on Kofi.

"Is this Kofi Donkor sitting at his favorite table, or a tokoloshe?"

Kofi stood and they embraced. Their closeness suggested a relationship that was more than friendship.

"You wish," Kofi replied. "Then you wouldn't have to pay back the stacks you owe me."

The woman let Kofi go with a frown. "Why do you always bring that up?"

"Because I'm a businessman," Kofi replied. "How have you been, Abena?"

"Better," Abena replied. "Merchants have been few and so has my customers. I hear there is war between Oyo and Asanteman. Which is the only reason I'm happy to see you."

She finally gave Omari her full attention. "And who is this beautiful man?"

"I've been called many things, but never beautiful," Omari said. "I'm Omari Ket."

"And I'm impressed," Abena replied. "You don't look like a bodyguard to me. You look like a man that could make more money on his back than on his feet. And don't take my compliment too seriously. It doesn't take much to be beautiful in this town. There are at least two goats here that are considered attractive by most."

Omari laughed. He liked this woman. Very much.

Abena was admiring Omari's arms when her hand went to her mouth.

"Is that what I think it is?"

Omari twisted his arm to make his ngisimaugi more visible.

"He's a Mikijen," Kofi said.

"Former Mikijen," Omari corrected.

"Daarila's balls!" Abena replied. "A Mikijen loses the ngisimaugi when they die or leave service. You're not dead, but your definitely not serving the Kiswala."

Omari decided to indulge in Abena's skepticism. He took out his knife, opened his left hand then cut his palm. Kofi and Abena watched as the ngisimaugi glowed and the cut healed.

"I told you," Kofi said. "I should have bet you, but you owe me enough money already."

Abena said nothing. Instead, she gave Omari a look that conveyed her intentions.

"It's good to see you, Kofi," she finally said. "I have a few barrels of beer that are about to go bad. I'll sell them to you at a discount or you can put the cost toward my debt."

"It's a deal."

Abena nodded at them both. She gave Omari one more long look then walked away.

"I think she's smitten with you," Kofi said.

"You don't have a problem with that?" Omari asked.

Kofi shrugged. "We had a thing long ago. It just business now. Not like you had to worry about me anyway. I don't relish having my back broken."

"It's not that serious," Omari said.

"So you say. You've been on the road a long time. I sense you're a man that doesn't go without often."

Omari grinned. "Your senses are correct."

The Akoben filled with customers as the market closed. Kofi's workers entered and gathered around his table, deciding to accept his offer. Servers appeared with meals and the barrels of beer Abena promised. If the brew was less than standard, it didn't show in the way Kofi and the others drank it. It was a bit stale for Omari's taste, but that was dulled by the fact that it was free.

The musicians arrived an hour after meals were served, taking up space in a corner set up specifically for them. The performers consisted of two djembe players, one kora and balafon player, and a jele strumming the akonting.

Lively music filled the tavern, the drunken patrons trying their best to dance. Omari was the center of attention at his table, where a game of oware took place. He won more than he lost, so much so that some patrons wouldn't play him. He was deep into a game when he felt a soft hand on his shoulder. He looked up into Abena's eyes.

"Winning again?" she asked.

"As always."

"Hah!" his opponent shouted. Abena's distraction had cost him the game. Omari frowned as he stood to make way for the next player.

"Thanks a lot," he said.

"Sometimes one must lose a battle to win the war," Abena replied. "Tell me, Omari Ket, can you dance?"

"It depends."

"On what?"

"Where I am. In Sati-Baa I'm perfect. In Kiswala, not so much."

"Come. I'll teach you how we dance in Asanteman."

Omari followed Abena onto the floor. He mimicked her moves and soon they were in perfect synch. Omari pulled Abena close and they continued to dance, their intentions obvious. Soon they were oblivious to everyone else.

"We need to go upstarts before we end up being the entertainment," Omari said.

"Yes. We do."

Abena led Omari upstairs then down a narrow hallway. They entered a room at the end of the passage, Abena's lair. It was a large, spacious dwelling adorned with objects from around Ki Khanga; Omari recognized a few things only found in Sati-Baa. As his eyes found Abena again, she was removing her dress.

"What are you waiting for? Permission?" Abena asked.

Omari answered by taking off his pants.

* * *

"Omari?"

"Hmm?"

"Wake up."

"Is it morning?"

"No."

"Then let's go back to sleep."

"You're not that special. I have to get back to work."

Omari opened his eyes to Abena putting on her clothes. He took a moment enjoying the view before clambering out of the large bed and searching for his garments. Abena was arranging her necklaces when the sound of drumming shook the floor.

"Dammit!" she exclaimed. Omari became alert.

"What is it? Is it an attack?"

"Worse," Abena replied. "It's Kola Kujo."

"Who?"

"Kola Kujo. He rules the land beyond the hills. His people think he's a god," Abena said. "Years ago, he won the Ibuthodili, so now he believes them. He thinks he's Eda blessed."

"That's not something you think," Omari said. "Either you are, or you aren't. And if you are, that's not exactly a blessing."

Abena stared at Omari. "You talk as if you know something I don't."

Omari shrugged. "Just something I heard during my days as a Mikijen."

The drumming became louder, singers chanting in time with the beat. The hired musicians began to play along.

"Stop it! Stop it!" Abena shouted. "I'm paying you!"

"Kola . . . Kujo . . . Ogun . . . Ye-O!"

Abena looked up toward the ceiling. "Ancestors, please protect my tavern! She hurried downstairs, Omari close behind. The tavern main floor had been rearranged. Tables and chairs had been pushed against the wall, creating a wide open space. Brightly garbed acrobats tumbled, inspired by a chorus of dancing singers and the crowd. Omari spotted Kofi and his crew along the edge, clearly enjoying the spectacle. Omari nodded his head to the beat and began clapping his hands. Abena pushed his head.

"What are you doing? They're destroying my place!"

"This Kola Kujo must be wealthy to manage all this," Omari said. "I'm sure he'll pay for whatever damages he creates."

"He didn't the last time," Abena replied. "It's the reason I owe Kofi stacks."

Four men wearing red loincloths and beaded caps entered the building carrying a litter filled with stacks. After them, another litter arrived, carrying the man known as Kola Kujo. The dancers became more vigorous, the drumming louder. The chorus chanted and the spectators, including Omari, joined in:

"Kola . . . Kujo . . . Ogun-Yeo!"

"Be quiet!" Abena said. "This will ruin me!"

The litter bearers carried Kola Kujo around the circle three times before taking him to the center and putting him down. Kola Kujo looked relatively young, a large man with short, cropped hair and a cowrie and leather band circling his head. He wore a leopard cape clasped with golden lion heads around his thick neck. A simple loincloth covered his privates, an ornate pair of leather sandals hugged his wide, long feet. Kola held out his jeweled ring encrusted hands as he smiled and nodded at the crowd. His eyes met Omari's and his smile widened. After a languorous turn, he lowers his arms to his sides. The music and dancing ceased.

"May Eda suckle you with blessings, and may Daarila guide your axe! I am Kola Kujo, greatest wrestler of all Ki Khanga. Today I issue a challenge to everyone inside these walls. Whoever can defeat me will be given these stacks. Are there any challengers?"

Omari eyed the stacks then shrugged. He had no need, especially if it meant fighting for them. He sized up Kola Kujo; although he seemed out of shape for a fighter, he gave the aura of a man who could handle himself. Still, he didn't look like someone who could have won the Ibuthodili. Omari had attended the event many times in his youth, mainly to steal from the unsuspecting attendees. Occasionally he would watch the matches, betting on fighters with his ill-gotten earnings. Most of the fighters he'd seen would put this Kola Kujo to shame, at least in physical appearance. But looks did not reveal the skill of a fighter; this was a fact Omari knew firsthand.

"I'll fight you!"

Odum, one of Kesi's porters, stepped onto the circle. The other porters cheered as the young laborer strutted, waving his hands to excite the crowd. Odum was lean and strong, but Omari doubted he could defeat Kola Kujo based on size alone. The drummers and dancers responded and soon the crowd chanted both men's names.

Odum! Kola! Odum! Kola!

Odum approached Kola and they clasped forearms.

"Thank you for your bravery," Kola said. "Not many men would face the champion of Ki Khanga."

"I have no idea who you are," Odum replied. "And I'm no easy mark. I've had quite a few brawls myself."

Kola grinned. "I respect your confidence. I can promise you this will not last long."

The two clasped arms. One of Kola Kujo's singers stepped forward with a small drum. She looked at them, then struck the drum.

Kola Kujo wasn't fast; he was sudden. His arms fell around Odum's waist and he lifted the man off his feet. With a grunt he flipped Odum upside down then slammed him on his head. Kola released the man then took a stance. Odum lay on the ground motionless; a healer rushed into the circle and check the still man.

"He's still alive," the healer said.

Kola Kujo's followers burst into chant.

"Kola . . . Kujo . . . Ogun-Yeo!"

Odum's friends ran to him and carried him out of the circle. Omari grinned. "He's quick, I'll give him that."

"Good," Abena replied. "Maybe he'll leave now."

Omari drank more beer. "I don't think so. Here comes another one."

The man entering the circle was massive. He moved with confidence as he removed his shirt and pants, revealing his loincloth. Unlike Odum, he made no effort to work the crowd. Instead, his dark eyes focused on Kola Kujo. Kola Kujo grinned as he looked at the man.

"You are a fighter," Kola said.

"I am," the man replied. "I am Assane. I was in Saati-Baa when you won the Ibuthodili. You were not the best fighter that day, yet you prevailed."

"I do not remember you," Kola replied. "Maybe you were not skilled enough to participate."

Kola's followers laughed, angering Assane.

"I was in training," Assane snapped. "You defeated my mentor and broke his spirit. He never recovered from the disgrace.

Because of you I had to train alone, praying for the day I would meet you. Today I am the man that will prove you are not the greatest. Today, I avenge my mentor Kankan Musa!"

Assane looked around as if he expected a roar of support. Instead there was only mumbling, a few burps, and a very loud fart.

Kola smiled. "That is not possible. I will savor defeating you."

The men clasped arms as Omari finished another beer.

"This is going to be good," he said.

Abena gave him a side-eye. "None of this is good. I hope he breaks Kola's neck."

"I think he will," Omari replied.

The woman with the drum returned. She eyed both men, then struck the drum.

Kola went for Assane's waist, but Assane punched him in the face. Kola staggered back stunned and his followers gasped. Assane charged while Kola struggled from the powerful blow. Assane stumbled, which gave Kola just enough time to recover. They locked arm, jerking and pulling each other, seeking advantage.

Omari grabbed another beer and gulped it down. "This beer is pretty good."

"I can tell you haven't had a good drink in a while," Abena said.

"I meant the fight, not the beer. The beer is terrible, but it's doing its job."

Abena's eyes narrowed and she smiled. "Don't drink too much. You have work to do tonight."

Omari grinned then pulled her into a kiss.

Kola and Assane were at a stalemate, both maneuvering for advantage but each thwarting the other with a counter. The crowd cheered them on, the sound deafening. Omari kept drinking, his amusement growing with each gourd emptied.

There was a loud crack followed by a howl. Assane fell to the ground holding his left arm which was bent at an odd angle. Kola Kujo stood over him like a triumphant statue.

"I submit!" Assane shouted.

"Of course you do," Kola Kujo replied. He raised his arms and his followers danced.

The healer ran to Assane, followed by two helpers. Together they guided Assane into the crowd. The young fighter glared as Kola as he left the circle; the fight was over, but Assane would return. Once again Kola Kujo's minions celebrated. Omari spotted a few in the crowd exchanging cowries. They had bet on the match, so there were winners and losers. Omari grabbed another beer and downed it in one draw. He wiped his lips with his sleeve, then took off his shirt.

"My turn," he said.

Abena grabbed his shoulder. "What are you doing?"

Omari grinned as he pulled away from Abena then sauntered toward the circle. The crowd clapped as they made way for him; Kola Kujo grinned as he approached.

"Mi-ki-jen! Mi-ki-jen!" Kofi shouted. The crowd quickly took up the chant. Omari waved his hands up and down, encouraging them. He danced up to Kola Kujo, swaying a bit before standing still.

"I was hoping you would come," Kola said. His eyes lowered to Omari's arms. "I've heard stories of the Mikijen. You are the greatest fighters in all Ki Khanga . . . with weapons."

Omari stumbled but quickly regained his composure.

"We are better with our hands, at least I am. I am from Saati Baa."

"Excellent! A street fighter! This should be interesting."

Omari winked. "More than you know."

Kola Kujo extended his arms but Omari did not take them. Instead he fell into the rhythmic steps known to all street fighters of the Shining Jewel. Kola followed Omari's foot movements for a moment, then advanced toward Omari.

Omari bent quickly, placing his left hand on the floor then whipping out a spinning kick that barely missed Kola's head. Had he been sober, the move would have been successful. Instead, Kola crashed into him as he rose and they tumbled to the floor. Kola tried to trap Omari in a hold, but Omari slipped from his grasp and returned to his feet. Two quick punches to the face rocked the wrestler, however the kick intended to knock the wind out of Kola was instead trapped under the big man's arm.

Kola brought his elbow down hard on Omari's shin and it cracked.

Omari held in his shout, slapping Kola's head instead. Kola loosened his grip and Omari grimaced as he yanked his leg free. The ngisimaugi warmed his back and arms as it healed his leg, Omari limping to the opposite side of the ring. Kola charged him, ready to take advantage of the broken bone. Omari managed to sidestep then pushed Kola into the crowd. By the time Kola fought his way out, Omari's leg was healed and the beer's effect was wearing off.

"Enough of this shit," Omari muttered.

Kola approached warily, seeking to grip arms. Omari reached out, but it was a ruse. As soon as they touched, Omari pounce forward with his knee aimed at Kola's head. But Kola had the same idea. Both knees hit their mark. Both men fell to the ground unconscious.

The stars were especially bright this night. Omari lay on his back admiring them, the night sounds of the bush distant yet pleasing. As he rested, the stars became brighter and the night sounds increased from subtle to deafening. His head ached and he reached for it with weak hands. Someone grabbed them both; a blurry image appearing before him in the shape of a woman.

"Eda?"

"You wish."

Omari's vision cleared to reveal Abena standing over him, surrounded by Kofi and the others. A cheer rose from them all as they lifted him to his feet. Omari's head swam and he reeled before being steadied by the others. His memory came back to him; he was about to knee Kola when he blacked out.

"Did I lose?" he asked.

"No, not all!" Kofi replied. "You won when you stood. Kola Kujo is still unconscious!"

Omari pushed the crowd aside. Kola Kudjo lay on his back surrounded by his wailing sycophants; their faces wet with tears. The healers worked frantically to revive the chief; their efforts slowed when they saw Omari. Kola's followers finally saw him and their lamentations increased. Omari staggered back to his table and took a small bag from his pouch. He ambled to Kola's prone form then pushed the healers aside. Kola's people shuffled away, looking at him in terror. Omari rolled his eyes. He opened the bag, leaned closed to Kola, then waved the bag under the chief's nose. Kola's head jerked away as he coughed then sat up. His eyes cleared as he frowned from the bag's piercing aroma. Kola finally recognized Omari and he grinned.

"Thank you," he said. "You were a worthy opponent."

Kola stood and his followers cheered. They rushed the man, pushing Omari aside. Omari sauntered away, looking for another beer.

"The stacks are yours," Kola shouted over the din. "You have defeated the greatest fighter of Ki Khanga. I look forward to our next meeting!"

"That will never happen," Omari said to himself, rubbing his throbbing forehead. Kesi, Abena and the others gathered around him, Abena with a beer gourd.

"I thought I had work to do tonight," Omari said.

"You do, but we must celebrate! This is the good beer."

Omari took the beer from her hand and drank it. "You're right. This is good."

The tavern rang with music and dancing. Abena took Omari's hand then gestured toward the stairs. Omari looked at Kesi then grinned.

"I'll see you in the morning . . . maybe."

Kesi laughed and patted him on the back. "Well done, Omari."

Abena leaned close then whispered into his ear.

"That's a lot of stacks," she said.

"They're yours," Omari replied. "Or maybe Kesi's?"

Abena kissed him hard. "Let's get you up those stairs!"

She looked at the crowd. "Drinks and food are on the house!"

The crowd roared and the house band played. Omari and Abena made their way to the stairs. Their celebration was about to begin.

Legacy

Omari guided the small riding bull down the narrow path into Oyo. He was entering a region at war, a place where he should not be, a detour on his way to claim the fortune waiting for him in Sati-Baa. This was not by choice; it was by command. He awoke two weeks ago in Abena's bed with an urge he could not suppress, a feeling that he'd never experienced before. As he donned his clothes and gathered his weapons, he saw his destination clearly, though he did not know the reason. Abena peppered him with questions but he did not answer. He could not. While walking to the village stables to secure a mount, the realization hit him. Eda had planted this seed in his mind, and he could not refuse. In the past she had teased, suggested, and threatened him into action. This time she gave him no choice, and it angered him.

Oyo and Asanteman were at war again, as were Mali and Fez, the Aux city-states and Menu-Kash, and Zimbabwa and Zambululand. For what, no one knew. Conflict raged across Ki Khanga as rivalries long dormant sprang to life. The loss of life and destruction was staggering, but the continent had endured such times and survived before. Yet there was something different this time. Adversaries fought with a ruthlessness that bordered on wholesale destruction. Times like these were idea for Kiswala, the merchants profiting from the scarcity of some items and the overabundance of others, conditions they were more than qualified to exploit. But even they were at war, attempting once again to establish themselves in their ancient homeland on the shores of Aux which they'd been driven from centuries ago.

None of this matter to Omari. As he dismounted near the banks of the river that served as a physical border between the two nations, he contemplated his situation. He did not want to make this journey, yet his urge to do so was involuntarily. He glanced upward, a snarl on his face.

"You could at least tell me why," he said to an absent Eda, expecting an answer. There was none.

Omari built a fire then warmed the dried meat he brought with him. The flesh was tough but flavorful; he'd definitely eaten worse. He gazed across the river and smirked as he recalled his last visit to Oyo. A bad night of gambling resulting in him taking a loan from the wrong person and finding himself presented as a gift the Oyo's Ngola. Instead of taking him into her harem, she sent him on a quest that if he succeeded, he would earn his freedom. The Ngola gave him to Izegbe, one of her best warriors, to make sure he performed his task. He chuckled when he remembered her, stern and beautiful face, amazing fighting skills, and a body that was firm yet supple and eager in his hands. She'd told him he 'wasn't as ugly as most men,' as good a complement he would ever get from a warrior of Oyo.

The sun began its descent below the ragged horizon. Omari rubbed his satisfied belly then decided he'd cross the river the next day. He waited for Eda's opinion, which usually came from a tightness in his chest, the place of the fatal wound she healed. There was nothing. He found a clear spot among a cluster of small trees to roost until the morning light.

No sooner did his head touch his headrest did he find himself running through the bush to the sounds of fighting. Before him was a heavily forested and steep hill. The mound seemed to writhe as hundreds of Oyo warriors charged upward, their war chants in the air. At the top of the hill was Izegbe, slaying her attackers with skill and brutality. Despite her expertise, the martial mass inched closer and closer. Just before she was overwhelmed, her eyes me Omari's. Her face was frozen in surprise as she was engulfed.

Omari sat up. This was not a dream. It was a portent of Izegbe's fate if he did not find her. She was trapped on a hill, surrounded by those who wished her dead. But why were the Oyo trying to kill not only one of their own, but someone who was well respected among them?

Omari realized he'd asked the question aloud, but there was no answer. Eda still refused to speak to him.

"What is she to you?" he asked Eda. There was no answer, just the calls of nocturnal bush animals.

Now that he knew his destination and who he was seeking, the urge to move increased. But he needed to sleep. If what he saw was true, he would need rest. He lay back down and eventually fell into a dreamless slumber.

* * *

Omari awoke the moment sunlight touched his skin. He packed his gear, mounted the bull and together they crossed the river into Oyo. His destination clear, Omari guided the bull down paths, roads, and through bush as if he'd traveled this route many a times. So far, he had encountered no war parties, but the conflict's devastation was always nearby. Bodies were scattered about, some in large numbers where battles had taken place. Villages, towns, and cities were destroyed; the inhabitants of those still standing either fleeing when they saw him or begging him for anything he could share. But he had nothing.

After a brief rest on the banks of a small lake, he continued on. His senses told him he was close to his destination. The hill appeared an hour later, looking exactly as it did in his dream. But unlike his dream, no warriors scaled its slopes. However, the smell of death surrounded him.

"Halt!"

Omari had been so immersed he didn't notice the Asanteman warriors approaching until it was too late. He counted five, four infantrymen carrying spears and one mounted on a Malian warhorse. The mounted man wore a chainmail shirt and kente kilt like the others; his head adorned by a metal helmet with a golden rank necklace resting in the center of his chest. He pointed at Omari with an iron sword, his hand gripping the golden pommel. Not only was he a man of rank; his sword told he was also a man of lineage.

The man guided his horse closer to Omari.

"Who are you? You're obviously not of Oyo, they despise men. And you're not a scavenger; you're too well dressed."

"I'm just a simple merchant passing through," Omari replied.

The man sucked his teeth. "That's a lie."

"He's a Mikijen," one of the other men said. "I can tell by his clothing. I traveled to Kiswala as a boy on a trading mission with my baba. They are mercenaries."

The rider's eyes widened. "Mercenaries? For whom do you work?"

Omari shook his head. "Like I said, I'm just passing through."

"This is a war zone," the commander said. "You could have chosen a safer route."

"I didn't know," Omari replied. "A different route would add months to my journey."

The rider tilted his head. "Where are you headed?"

Omari was becoming annoyed. "You ask a lot of questions."

The commander shook his sword. "And if you wish to live, you will answer them."

The soldiers lowered their spears to attack position. Omari rolled his eyes as if unconcerned. The spear wielders were no threat; they were probably conscripts who were taught a few tricks with their weapons then sent to fight. Their commander was another matter. Omari could tell by his scars and his demeanor that he was a fighter.

"Sati-Baa," Omari finally said.

The rider reached into his bag and took out a small pouch. He tossed it to Omari.

"Gold dust," he said. "There's another bag for you if you take care of a problem at the top of this hill."

A bag of gold dust was of little value to the Asanteman, but outside its borders it was almost as valuable as kipande.

"What's at the top of the hill?" Omari asked.

"A situation holding a sword," the commander replied.

Omari grinned. Izegbe was holding her own. He tossed the gold dust pouch in the air then caught it. "I'll see what I can do."

"See, I told you!" the spearman said. "He's a Mikijen!"

"Shut up, Ato," the commander barked. He turned his attention back to Omari. "Kill her then bring back her head."

Omari pressed his heels into the bull's side. The bull bellowed then trotted toward the trail.

"I'll try," he said.

The ride up the hill turned out to be a cumbersome journey. Izegbe had chosen her hold out well. Anyone ascending the mount on foot would be exhausted when they reached the top, and Izegbe would attack them as soon as she could. It was a good thing he was coming in peace. He didn't feel like being stabbed.

The spear hit him in the shoulder, knocking him off the bull. "Cleave!" he shouted before crashing onto the ground. Izegbe appeared seconds later, looming over him with her battle axe held high, ready to deliver a killing blow. Omari kicked her feet from under her as he pulled the spearhead from his shoulder. They both sprang from the ground as if it was a hot iron kettle. He snatched his sword free then knocked Izegbe's axe out of her hand.

"Izegbe! It's me! Omari!"

Izegbe yelled. She drew her machetes then attacked. Footwork and desperation kept Omari's wounds to a minimum.

"Enough of this!" he hissed.

Omari feinted, lowering his weapons as if exhausted. Izegbe rushed in for the kill but ended up on Omari's shoulder as he charged into her then lifted her off the ground. He slammed her down hard, her weapons flying from her grip. Omari pinned her arms down with his knees then pulled his head away to avoid her gnashing teeth.

"Izegbe! Look at me! It's Omari!"

Something hard hit the back of his head, stunning him. He fell off Izegbe, his right hand going instinctively to where he was struck. He turned around to see a girl standing near him with a war club in her hand and determination on her face. She raised the club.

"Nourbese, no!"

Izegbe darted by Omari then grabbed the girl by the wrist. The girl tried to jerk away, but Izegbe's grip was like a trap.

"No, he's not an enemy," Izegbe said.

The ngisimaugi warmed and the head pain subsided. Izegbe stared at Omari bewildered.

"She said she would send someone. I didn't believe her at first, but she kept coming to me in my dreams until I could not deny her. I never suspected it would be you."

"If by she you mean Eda, she has been sparse with her words," Omari replied.

"It was Eda," Izegbe said.

Omari's looked at the girl as he picked up his sword. "Who is the little warrior?"

Izegbe hugged her. "Nourbese. She is my daughter."

Omari frowned at the girl, reflecting the stern look on her face. Then he saw something familiar, something in the shape of her eyes, in the curve of her nose, thickness of her brows . . .

"This is my daughter!"

Izegbe jumped in front of the girl. "No! She is mine!"

"And mine," Omari said. The realization hit him harder than Nourbese's club. It wasn't that he'd never thought of children; there had been many women in his life, so there was always the possibility of pregnancy. But he never imagined he would be standing before his child like this.

"How did . . ."

"Don't be stupid," Izegbe said. "I slept with you to have a child. Despite your dull wit, you are a strong man with natural abilities. We were a good physical match. You were never meant to know because it is our way. But now you do. But it doesn't matter. She is mine."

Nourbese stepped closer to Omari, a curious look on her face. The news seemed to be just as shocking to her as it was to him.

"This is my baba?"

"Yes," Izegbe said. "There is something else Omari," Izegbe said. She waved toward Nourbese. "Come here."

Nourbese walked back to Izegbe.

"Turn your back and lift your shirt."

Nourbese scowled. "Do I have to?"

"He must know."

Nourbese did as she was told. In the center of her back, was a ngisimaugi. Omari's mouth fell open.

"Daarila's beard! This is impossible!"

"Why?" Izegbe asked. "You have one."

Omari knelt near Nourbese, studying the mark on her back.

"The ngisimaugi is not a birthmark, it is a tattoo given to a Mikijen as their final initiation. It gives us our healing powers, and it fades away when we die or leave the Mikijen."

It was Izegbe's turn to be dumbfounded. "So how can this be? And why do you still possess yours?"

"This is Eda's doing," Omari said, his tone unpleasant. He looked up, searching about with his eyes. "Are we pawns in your game?" he shouted. "What are you doing to me? To my daughter?"

Omari felt his chest tighten around the scar of the wound that should have taken his life. His breath shortened, his heart pounding against his ribs. He fell to one knee, clutching his shirt. He'd gone too far. Izegbe rushed to him.

"What is wrong?"

"I'm being punished," Omari struggled to say. He looked up and managed to smile. "I know, I know. You can stop now." Omari winced as a final sharp pain coursed through him just before the chest pains subsided. He struggled to his feet, Izegbe and Nourbese looking at him as if he had three heads.

"Eda blesses you," Izegbe whispered.

"I guess you could call it that. I wouldn't. Why are you here, Izegbe? Shouldn't there be other warriors with you?"

Izegbe lowered her head. "I am no longer favored by the Ngola."

"What happened?"

Izegbe glanced at Nourbese. "When the Ngola discovered Nourbese's abilities, she wanted to take her and train her to be one of her elite guards."

"Isn't that normal for Oyo?" Omari asked. "It's an honor, I believe."

"It is," Izegbe replied. "But I did not wish it. When the warriors came for her, I refused. There was a fight. Lives were lost. I took Nourbese and we hid in the bush."

Omari shook his head. "I did not see you as one who would defy the Ngola."

"I did not see that either. There was something else."

"What?"

Izegbe took a deep breath. "I knew I was pregnant by you before our mission for the Ngola was complete. By our tradition, I should have killed you."

Omari's eyes went wide. "Daarila's axe!"

"The Ngola spared me for my transgression but demoted me to a common warrior. But fleeing with Nourbese could not be ignored. She decreed I was to be killed and Nourbese brought back to her. But then the Asanteman invaded."

"The men I encountered paid me to kill you," Omari said. "I thought they were Asanteman, but they must be assassins sent by the Ngola. Let's gather your things. Eda has shown me where we're going. It will be a long journey. Hopefully, I can secure you horses."

Nourbese's eyes widened. "Mama! Someone is coming!"

Omari and Izegbe crouched instinctively, their eyes searching the foliage for ambushers. Nourbese closed her eyes, her forehead wrinkling.

"They are coming up the road," Nourbese said." Thirteen of them."

"How does she know this?" Omari asked.

"It is another one of her talents," Izegbe answered. "The Ngola does not know of this."

Omari looked at his daughter with pride in his eyes before turning his attention back to the bush. "It must be the men I encountered."

"They followed you," Izegbe said.

"Not exactly," Omari replied. "They paid me to kill you."

"They come to make sure you did the deed," Izegbe said. She peeked over the brush and frowned. "They are too close. It is too late to run."

Omari drew his sword and dagger. "I agree."

Izegbe placed her hand on Nourbese's shoulder. "Stay here, stay quiet."

"But I want to help!"

"No!" Izegbe shouted.

Nourbese folded her arms across her chest and glared at Izegbe.

"Such disrespect," Izegbe commented. "I think she gets that from you."

"Probably," Omari said. "Does she also prefer beer to palm wine?"

Izegbe almost laughed. "Be quiet, stupid man."

The assassins broke the horizon, the horse rider leading. Omari looked about until he found the bull a few strides away.

"I'll take the rider. Can you handle the others?"

Izegbe grinned, her filed teeth exposed. "I look forward to it."

Omari sprinted to the bull, climbed onto its back then jerked the reins.

"Hut!"

The bull snorted then broke into a run, Omari guiding it toward the assassins. The horse rider grinned as they attacked, a crooked smile on his face. The horse was much larger than the bull, but the rider overestimated his advantage. As the Malian stallion rose on its hind legs to attack, the bull drove its horns into the horse's torso. The horse screeched in pain then fell aside, taking the rider with it. Omari leapt from the bull, sword and dagger drawn. The rider climbed to his feet, sword drawn as well. They fell onto each other with skilled fury, two men well versed in violence.

Omari spun away from a thrust meant for his abdomen, swinging his sword at the man's neck and barely missed beheading him. The mercenary attacked again, Omari parrying with his dagger then driving his foot into the man's shin. The mercenary opened his mouth to scream and Omari filled it with his sword.

Omari turned to see Nourbese running toward hill crest with a warclub, two warriors in pursuit. Izegbe was fending off other warriors, but Omari knew she would want him to save the child. He ran after the men, trying to catch up with them as they reached the summit and disappeared over the edge. A moment later one of the men tumbled down the slope, cursing as he held his left eye. Omari stabbed his throat as he ran by him.

He crested the summit to a sight that would have been humorous if it wasn't so deadly. Nourbese stood like a warrior, a fierce look on her face as she spun her warclub over her head. Frustration showed on the warrior's face.

"I should kill you, little monkey," he said. "But I'll get more cowries for you alive."

Omari crept up to the man then drove his sword through him. The warrior fell aside, and Nourbese's face went from defiance to relief. She dropped her club and ran to Omari. He let go of his sword and caught him in his arms. The bond was instant, sweeping over him like the warmth of a dry season sun. He closed his eyes as he squeezed her.

"It's okay, daughter. I have you."

"Omari!"

Omari turned to see Izegbe stalking toward him, a grim look on her face, her clothes smeared with blood.

"We have no time for this. We have to go."

Omari held on to Nourbese. "I know. We leave now. I know our destination. A place where you both can be safe."

Izegbe looked dumbfounded. "We have to leave Oyo?"

"Yes." Eda guided Omari's words. "The Ngola is not the only one hunting you. There are . . . other forces after you as well."

"What forces?" Izegbe asked.

"I don't know," Omari admitted. "I just know that you will be safer in Wadantu."

Izegbe was about to dispute him but she stopped. She closed her eyes, then opened them with understanding.

"Yes. It is where we must go."

"It will be long journey," Omari warned. "And we will be hunted every step of the way."

Izegbe grinned. "I am not worried. I have you to fight with me, and you are better than most men."

Omari rolled his eyes. "So you keep telling me."

Omari found his bull grazing beside the corpse of the war horse. He put Nourbese on the saddle, and they descended the hill.

"Which way must we go?" Izegbe asked.

"East," Omari replied. "We must find a village and change our clothes. We must become a family."

"Why?" Izegbe asked.

"Because we're being hunted and we don't want to be obvious. We'll buy clothes at the next village."

"Anyone in Oyo will recognize what I am," Izegbe replied.

"Which is why you'll stay hidden."

Izegbe folded her arms and tapped her foot.

"What?" Omari said.

"You are asking me to take orders from you," she replied. "I do not take orders from a man."

"I'm not ordering you," Omari said. "I'm interpreting Eda's wisdom. Plus I know a few things about getting out of trouble."

"You are a dishonest man," Izegbe said.

"Wait, I didn't say that!"

"If you have skills in avoiding trouble, it means you are one who often does things that require escape."

Omari couldn't argue. Izegbe was already getting on his nerves, and they had a long journey ahead.

"Yes. I'm a dishonest man when I need to be," Omari confessed. "I have lied, cheated, and stolen my entire life. And I am particularly good at all of them. Which is why I know I can get us to Wadantu. So are we going to keep discussing this until someone finds us and kills us all, or do we keep moving?"

"We keep moving," Izegbe said. "Although fighting and dying would be the honorable thing."

"Eda does not wish it," Nourbese said. "She told me."

Omari and Izegbe eyes went wide.

"She spoke to you?" Izegbe asked.

Nourbese nodded.

"When?" Omari asked.

"When I was running," Nourbese answered. "She told me do not worry, because I was special to her. She said that both of you would die before you let anything happen to me. I asked her why you would do such a thing, and she said because I was important to her, so you had no choice."

Omari couldn't deny Nourbese's words, and Izegbe's expression showed her agreement.

"There is a village not far from here," Izegbe said. "We can get clothing and supplies there."

"Lead the way," Omari said.

It took them a few hours to reach their first destination. Luckily, it was untouched by the war.

"I'll go to the village just in case someone might recognize you," Omari said.

Izegbe and Nourbese stayed back in the bush, Omari walking down the road with without his weapons. A group working on the thorn fence surrounding the village spotted him and ran away yelling a waring. Moment later the village garrison trotted toward Omari with spears lowered. Their chief led them, a tall woman whose girth made Izegbe look small. She wore a long patterned skirt with an old leather breastplate, brandishing a sword.

"I should kill you where you stand, Asanteman!" she shouted.

Omari raised his hands and lowered his head. "I'm no Asanteman. Just a merchant who has lost his way. All I wish are clothes for my wife and daughter and provisions."

"I don't see anyone," the chief replied.

Omari gestured toward the bush. "They hide in the bush."

The chief moved closer and the garrison followed. "Women are slaves to their men outside of Oyo," the chief said. "Your family should be liberated."

"Please. I am not one of those men. My family means everything to me. If we could . . ."

Omari saw the chief's hand move in plenty of time to block it, but he allowed it to strike his face. He stumbled backwards, then looked at the chief with false shock.

"Women!" the chief called out. "Come!"

Izegbe emerged from the bush leading the bull with Nourbese on its back. Omari assessed his situation they neared. He would have a hard time fighting his way out of this one, especially if Izegbe decided to take her chances in Oyo. At the same time, if the chief recognized who Izegbe was, there would be a fight regardless.

The chief's expression transformed from stern to shock. The other warriors reacted the same. By the time Izegbe reached them they were kneeling, their foreheads touching the ground.

"Honored Ahosi," the chief sputtered. "We did not know!"

Izegbe touched the chief's head and she stood.

"Who are you? Izegbe asked.

"Wogbe," the chief said.

"Sister Wogbe, we need clothing and supplies for our journey. Can you give them to us?"

"Of course," Wogbe replied.

"Good. You will be paid, of course."

Wogbe shook her head. "That is not necessary. It is our honor."

Wogbe was about to walk away then turned around. "Honored Mother, I have a question."

"What is it?"

"Why did you send this man to speak for you?"

"The war has made me wary," Izegbe replied. "I do not know who I can trust. When you hit him, I knew you were true to the Ngola."

Wogbe smiled. "I see. I will see to your needs immediately." She gestured at two of her warriors.

"Gebeda and Dokpe, go to the village and bring back clothing and food for our Honored Mother."

The women nodded then ran toward the village. Wogbe and the others sat then invited Izegbe to join them. Izegbe took Nourbese from the bull and they all sat in a circle. The women shared their provisions with Izegbe and Nourbese, their conversation light and easy. Omari was ignored, which was fine by him. He needed the rest and wasn't much for small talk. He was hungry, but he could wait.

The warriors returned with bags filled with clothing and gourds of provisions. The bags and gourds were attached to the bull and Nourbese was helped onto its back. Only then did one of the women come to Omari, frowning as if he smelled bad. He probably did. She tossed him a small gourd then spit at his feet. Though he hadn't visited Oyo in years, it was comforting to know that some things hadn't changed.

They left the village, continuing their journey east.

"That was unpleasant," Omari said.

Izegbe laughed. "You handled yourself well. I was worried when Wogbe slapped you."

Omari shrugged. "I've suffered worst for a ruse. It was good she didn't know of the bounty."

Izegbe grinned. "She knew. Woge is a woman of honor. She will give us a few days before she reports us to the Ngola. We must be gone from Oyo before then."

They traveled until dusk then set up camp not far from the river. They ate a light meal then went to bed for the night, Izegbe and Nourbese sleeping together a distance from Omari. He understood their wariness. Eda had not made her intentions clear, and it had been years since Izegbe had seen him. Omari built a soft place to lay down, gathering fallen leaves and underbrush then covering it with his thick blanket. He hated sleeping outdoors; his recent wealth had allowed him to rest in some of the best inns in Ki Khanga with many willing companions. He couldn't think of a worse situation.

He dug through his bags and found his money pouch. He still possessed a good amount of coins, cowries, gold dust, and stacks, in addition to the valuable anklet. Still, his funds could use a bit of boosting. He would have to do something about that once he took Izegbe and Nourbese to their destination.

The sun descended below the horizon, darkness settling in around them. The calls and cries of night beasts rose in the distance, eventually lulling Omari to sleep. He dreamed immediately, finding himself in a large soft bed, the smell of perfumes bringing a smile to his face. A warm presence pressed against him; he opened his eyes to see Aisha, her arms slithering around his waist.

"So warm," a feminine voice said. *"So warm."*

The arms tightened around Omari.

"Not too tight lover," he whispered.

"So warm," Aisha replied. *"So, so warm."*

Omari's ribs ached. "Aisha!"

"So warm. So warm!"

Omari's eyes popped opened. Thick tentacles constricted around him, his right arm pinned against his body. He attempted to move his legs but they were pressed together. Nourbese's scream ripped through the darkness, Izegbe's curses audible in the background. Omari reached out with his left hand, desperately seeking anything to help break the grip squeezing the air out of him. His palm landed on a large rock;

Omari gripped it then slammed it against the slimy appendage dragging him toward the river.

The river exploded and Omari was flung into the air. He crashed against a tree, tumbling through its branches then hitting the ground. The ngisimaugi warmed as he stood and sprinted toward his pack. Something large and dark loomed at the river's edge, its multiple eyes emitting their own eerie light. Omari saw Izegbe and Nourbese sliding toward the thing, Izegbe struggling to free herself, Nourbese still screaming.

Omari neared his weapons. A tentacle flashed out, striking him in his face. He spun to the ground then jumped back to his feet. Another tentacle grabbed his ankle as he found the hilt of his sword. He cut the tentacle from his leg then charged toward the thing. The creature responded, releasing Izegbe and Nourbese then attacking Omari with them all. Omari swung his blade wildly, cutting some tentacles while others struck and grabbed at his body. The creature's eye light illuminated his body while its tentacles attempted to grab his sword.

A spear appeared at the edge of his sight and plunged into one of the creature's eyes. It screeched as its light shifted. Izegbe ran toward the thing, a bundle of throwing spears in her left hand, another ready to launch in her right hand. A tentacle struck out, hitting her in the chest and knocking her to the ground.

Omari took advantage of the beast's distraction. He charged forward, driving his sword into the center of the creature's head. It shuddered then wrapped all its tentacles around Omari as it retreated into the river. Omari could not break free; all he could do was twist the sword hoping the creature would succumb to its wounds. Water flowed around and up his legs then covered him as the creature sank into the river. Terror gripped Omari: drowning was one thing the ngisimaugi could not save him from. He held his breath as he worked the sword side to side, widening the wound. The tentacles loosened then fell away, the creature's eye light dimming to darkness.

Omari swam desperately through the black waters, his breath about to give way. His head broke the surface; his mouth opened instinctively then filled with water. Omari choked for what seemed like forever before he could compose himself enough to swim toward the shore. He dragged himself onto the dirt then rolled on his back, coughing out the rest of the water.

Rough hands touched his face. He opened his eyes to Izegbe kneeling beside him, her hands holding his cheeks. Nourbese stood beside her. Their faces filled with relief.

"That was not fun," Omari said.

Izegbe frowned as Nourbese giggled.

He sat up, then coughed some more. "I think we should move away from the river."

Izegbe helped Omari walk to his resting place and gather his things. By the time they finished packing Izegbe and Nourbese's things, Omari had recovered. They made their way through the brush as best they could in darkness, determined to distance themselves from the river and whatever other surprises it might contain. They stopped at the top of a small hill. It was a good spot that gave the higher ground advantage in case there were others seeking them. Izegbe prepared a place for Nourbese, singing softly to her until she fell asleep. Omari sat with his back against a small tree, massaging his ribs as the ngisimaugi slowly pushed the pain away. Izegbe sat beside him.

"What was that thing?" Omari asked.

"A Swimming Lover," Izegbe replied. "It is said to live in the deep rivers, where the waters are so dark creatures carry their own light. It captures its victims with its tentacles, crushing them as it brings pleasures with dreams. You are lucky you woke. We all are."

Omari grimaced as he sat up straight. "I dreamed of Aisha."

"Who is she?" Izegbe asked.

"A close friend from long ago. I hope to see her again when I reach Sati-Baa. Who did you dream of?"

Izegbe's eyes softened. "No one you would know."

"You hurt my feelings," Omari said. "I was sure it was me."

"Ha."

Omari frowned. "Was I that bad?"

"There was one," she said. "His name was Manu. We met during the Sorghum festival in Kenja. I and three of my sisters infiltrated the gathering to capture seed. I saw him wrestling for a bag of cowries and two goats. He won easily, for he was tall with thick muscles and the quickness of a mamba. After his victory, I approached him and told him I wanted to lay with him." Izegbe's eyes took a faraway look then she laughed.

"What?" Omari asked.

"He was embarrassed," Izegbe continued. "He ran away like a boy. I should have left him alone, but it was amusing to me. I kept following him until he finally confronted me. He wanted to know why I kept following him, and I told him again I wanted to lie with him. He finally confessed that he had never been with a woman."

It was Omari's turn to laugh. "I would have done many things, but I wouldn't have run away."

"You are like most men," Izegbe replied. The tone in her voice let Omari know her words were not a compliment.

"So you laid with him," Omari said.

"I did," Izegbe said. "It was different. He was . . . tender. Careful. We both found it extremely pleasurable. Then I left."

"And that was it?" Omari asked. "You never saw him again."

"Of course not!" Izegbe snapped. "I am a warrior of Oyo. His seed did not take, but I think about him often."

"So you were in love with him?"

Izegbe scowled. "I did not say that. Go to sleep. I'll take first watch."

Omari didn't argue. He fell asleep as soon as his head touched his headrest.

* * *

The smell of sorghum and goat broke Omari from his slumber. He sat up and inspected his body. The bruises were gone, but there was still some soreness. Izegbe and Nourbese sat in front of a fire, an iron pot suspended over the flames. Izegbe looked at him then spoke to Nourbese. The girl stood then walked to him.

"Good morning, baba," she said. "Mama said to come. The stew is almost ready."

Omari sat motionless. "Baba?"

Nourbese nodded. "Mama said that is what Asanteman children call their male parents. She said I should call you that until we leave Oyo."

Omari's face warmed with a feeling he'd never experienced before. He grinned at Nourbese, and she smiled back.

"Baba," he said. "Okay, daughter. Let's join Mama."

Omari and Nourbese joined Izegbe at the fire.

"It's a lovely day wife," Omari said. Izegbe frowned at the as she gave him a bowl.

"Eat."

Omari sat beside Izegbe then kissed her cheek. She shoved him over onto his side and Nourbese laughed.

"Your mama is in a bad mood today," Omari said.

"Do that again and I'll stab you," Izegbe replied. She filled Omari's bowl, then Nourbese's before filling her own.

"Where do we go now?" Izegbe asked.

"We'll continue east until we reach the sea," Omari said. "We'll buy passage on a merchant or fishing ship sailing to Kongo. Once we reach Kongo, we won't be far from Wadantu."

"How long will that take?"

"Two weeks. Three at the most."

"And when we reach Wadantu?"

"Eda will tell us, I hope."

They finished the meal then set on their way, taking turns riding the bull. For three days they traveled in peace, occasionally passing a lone traveler or a small village where they would trade and buy supplies. The war seemed to have bypassed this region; the people were less wary yet still curious about an Oyo woman and her daughter traveling with a man. Izegbe told them he was her servant and though many accepted her explanation, the situation was still odd.

It was on the fourth day of their journey that the war once again intruded on their journey. They heard the fighting in the distance, the familiar cacophony of clashing metal and shields, cries of anger and pain.

They were turning away when Asanteman warriors charged up the path toward them. Omari and Izegbe drew their weapons and met the warriors with deadly fury. Together they quickly defeated them.

Omari sheathed his sword and dagger. "Let's go before more . . ."

Izegbe ran to the bull. She pushed Nourbese back then jumped onto its back, driving her heels into its sides. The bull bellowed then charged down the path toward the battle. Nourbese clutched Izegbe's waist as they rode away, looking back at Omari, her face twisted with fear.

"Cleave!" Omari sprinted after them, loading his hand cannon along the way. The path widened to reveal a grim scene. Asante and Oyo bodies littered an open field; the remaining warriors locked in bitter battle. Asanteman warriors surrounded a small group of ahosi, the women fighting furiously to hold them back. They were vastly outnumbered; their defeat was inevitable. The Asanteman fighters were so focused on the ahosi that Izegbe's attack caught them completely by surprise. The bull gored the startled warriors as Izegbe cut left and right with her machetes. Nourbese clung to Izegbe, trying her best not to fall.

Omari came into range. He fired his handgun, the scattered shot taking down four warriors. The blast drew attention; a group of warriors broke from the main group and ran in his direction.

"Shit!" Omari turned and ran. He hoped Izegbe would follow his lead. If they drew enough of the warriors away, the ahosi could turn the tide. But she did not. She seemed determined to fight her way to her sisters.

"Damn it to the Cleave!" Omari spun around and attacked. He drove his foot into the chest of the first man to reach him, knocking back into the man behind him. He sidestepped the warrior charging around the other, slashing the warrior's thigh as he evaded him. The next man he met head on, locking swords with him as he drove his dagger into his neck. Omari's battle instinct took over, years of fighting guiding his movements. When the fighting subsided his mind cleared; he was surrounded by dead and dying warriors, his body covered with his own blood and the blood of others. The ngisimaugi pulsed, his wounds healing as he scanned the killing ground. Izegbe dismounted the bull as her sister warriors trudged toward her. Nourbese sat on the bull, her mouth agape, her body trembling.

"Daarila's balls," Omari said as he hurried to them.

The handful of warriors gathered around Izegbe. Their faces were not friendly. One fighter stepped forward, a stout woman with rank bands on her biceps. She nodded at Izegbe, and Izegbe nodded back.

"Izegbe. Thank you for your help, my sister," the woman said.

"Oseye. We fight as one," Izegbe replied.

Oseye glanced at her warriors and they shifted, their stances less friendly. The leader shared a predatory smile.

"The Ngola will be happy to see Nourbese. Because you have helped us, we will allow you to leave with your man."

Omari broke into a run as Izegbe stood between the ahosi and the bull.

"You will not take her," Izegbe said.

The leader was about to speak when Izegbe cut off her head. The other warriors stood frozen, their shocked expressions shifting to fury as they fell on Izegbe. Omari crashed into them, striking quickly and deadly. In moments, the fight was over. Izegbe staggered back, her eyes wide. She turned to Omari, her eyes burning with hate as she raised her machetes. Omari stepped back.

"They were going to kill you!" he said.

Izegbe took a fighting stance and bare her teeth. Omari prepared to defend himself.

"Did you think they were actually going to let us go?" he said.

Nourbese ran to Izegbe and wrapped her arms around her waist. "Mama no!"

The fury in Izegbe's eyes faded with Nourbese's plea. She lowered her machetes then let them fall from her hands. Izegbe sank to her knees, covered her face, and cried. Nourbese knelt beside her and cried as well.

Omari walked up, placing his hand on Izegbe's shoulder. She shrugged it way.

"We must go," he said. "If you weren't in enough trouble, you are now."

Izegbe stood, then wiped her face. She sheathed her machetes then picked up Nourbese, placing her on the bull's back. She glared at Omari.

"What kind of spirit is Eda that she would have me kill my own kind?"

"You'll have to ask her," Omari replied. "But you had no choice. I feel Daarila's hand in this."

Omari's eyes met Nourbese's. The sadness he saw in her eyes was painful to see, but there was nothing he could do about it. Omari had known much worse when he was her age; at least she had two people and a deity watching over her. He would have given anything to have had half as much. He grabbed the bull's reins, and they continued to the east.

*   *   *

The trio moved in silence for the next week. The last battle seemed to have broken Izegbe's spirit. She spoke only when spoken to and did the minimum attending to Nourbese's needs. Omari was at a loss for words. He didn't know how to interact with a child, and he didn't know what to do to bring Izegbe out of her mood. He occupied himself with cleaning his weapons and songs while Izegbe and Nourbese kept to themselves.

After sharpening his sword for the one hundredth time, Omari went into his pack and took out his oware game. It had been weeks since he'd played, and he missed the excitement of winning cowries from unsuspecting opponents. He was filling the pods with seeds when he heard a small voice.

"What is that?"

He turned to see Nourbese standing behind him, her eyes wide with curiosity.

"It's a game," Omari replied. "One that I'm particularly good at. Would you like me to show you how to play?"

"Yes!" Nourbese sat beside him, leaning against his arm.

"We call it oware where I'm from," Omari said. "I've heard it called other names such as mancala, ban-ban, and khalah."

Omari explained the rules to Nourbese as he moved the seeds from pod to pod.

"You understand?" he asked.

"I think I do."

Omari smirked. "Only one way to find out. Let's play."

Omari and Nourbese played the remainder of the day. By sunset not only was Nourbese proficient, but she had also beaten Omari more than once. Frustration was clear on Omari's face.

"By the Cleave!" he shouted as he lost another game. "You must be Eda blessed. No one has beaten me like this!"

"I told you she was special."

Izegbe sat beside Nourbese and gave her a hug.

"Mama! Baba taught me to play oware. I'm better than him now!"

"No you're not," Omari said. "You're just lucky."

"Then let's make it interesting," Izegbe said. She reached into her pouch and took out a handful of cowries. "I bet you five cowries that Nourbese wins the next game."

Omari took out an equal amount of cowries. "Accepted!"

Izegbe leaned close to Nourbese. "Make your mama proud."

The game began and Nourbese won.

"Best two out of three," Omari said. He placed more cowries between them.

"Okay!" Nourbese said.

Omari took the second game and he celebrated with a fist pump. His joy was short-lived. Nourbese took the third game and his cowries.

"I can't believe this!" Omari said. He flipped the board, the seeds scattering everywhere. Izegbe and Nourbese celebrated by dancing and chanting.

"I'm going to sleep," Omari said. "I'll see you both in the morning." Omari found a clear area and set up his bed. He looked at Izegbe and Nourbese still dancing and smiled. The game had lifted their spirits. He'd lost deliberately for that reason. Nourbese was truly their daughter, smart, skilled, and proud. If he ever imagined having a family, it would be like this. The thought brought realization with it. It was then he understood Eda's purpose. With Nourbese, there was someone in this world he cared for more than himself. The thought pleased and terrified him.

Tai-mzoga circled in the sky, gliding on the strong winds from the Sati Baa sea. The stench of death and smoke rode those winds as well, sketching an odoriferous portrait of the upcoming scene. Omari, Izegbe, and Nourbese followed the road leading to Adumadan, Oyo's sole port city on the Sati-Baa Sea and the origin of the river of the same name. The ruins came into view minutes later, a killing ground long abandoned to scavengers. The smoke from fires had long dissipated. Single jackals roamed the silent streets seeking remains; packs of hyenas scattering when they came near. Omari said nothing, for he would be speaking the obvious; the Ahosi were losing this war. Only the Alaafin's mercy could save them and based on the history between the nations such a clemency would not happen.

"Don't worry," Omari said. "We should be able to find a dhow at the port," Omari said. "I'm a decent baharia. We'll sail to Kenja, then walk the rest of the way to Wadantu."

Izegbe nodded, her eyes scanning the terrible scene. Nourbese said nothing, clinging to Izegbe with tears in her young eyes. It was a scene Omari had seen many times; in some cases he marched with those who caused such destruction. Time had hardened his heart to such things, but seeing the effect it had on Izegbe and Nourbese made him sad for them.

Omari was relieved when they reached the docks. The damage and smell were less pronounced; Omari suspected the merchants were able to make their escape before the Asanteman calvary reached them. There were a few dhows still moored. Omari inspected them, eventually finding one in good enough condition to take them across the sea.

"I'll have to scavenge a few items from the other boats, but otherwise we have what we need."

He scanned the area and saw a small building, most likely the home of the dock master. Omari pointed at it.

"We'll settle there until we're ready to sail," he said.

"How long will that be?" Izegbe asked.

"Two days, maybe three," Omari replied. "Not long. I'll get started. Take Nourbese to the home and rest. I'll be along later."

Izegbe nodded. She placed Nourbese on the bull and they went to the home. Omari searched the dhow he chose and found fishing lines, hooks, and a casting net. Whoever once owned the boat were fishers. They most likely used the net to catch baitfish and then used them to catch bigger prey in the deep waters of the lake, most likely spinfish. The thought of the succulent fish made his mouth water. It would be a welcomed break from dried food and bush meat, but they had no time. He would have to settle for whatever he could catch in the shallow dingy water of the docks.

He was done rigging the dhow by nightfall. The work had drained him, but at least he had caught a few fish, which meant a fresh meal. He cleaned the fish by the shore, humming a song from long ago, a tune his mother used to sing when preparing their meals. Omari had few good memories from his childhood and hearing her voice during those moments was one of them. He gathered pieces of wood to make a fire once he reached the house; if he was lucky there was a firepit inside for cooking.

Omari opened the door. Nourbese sat on the floor, her eyes wet with tears.

"Where is Izegbe?" Omari asked.

"She's gone," Nourbese said, then cried.

Omari dropped to his knees and hugged her.

"What do you mean, gone?"

Nourbese handed Omari a rolled up piece of parchment. He let Nourbese go, then flattened the paper on the floor. It was written in trade script.

I cannot leave my sisters this way. The Ngola needs every one of us if we are to win. Take Nourbese to Wadantu. I will meet you when I am done here, or if Eda wishes it. Goodbye, Omari. You are not so bad for a man.

Omari wanted to ripped the parchment apart, but sharing his foul mood was the last thing needed. He thought of chasing after her, but she had the bull and a day's head start. As his emotions settled, he realized Eda let her leave, which meant whatever was happening was meant to be. Nourbese was his responsibility now.

Nourbese's crying had waned, though her tears still flowed. Omari was struggling for the right words when she spoke.

"Mama told me to be brave," she said. "She told me I could trust you, that you would never let anything or anyone hurt me as long as you lived. She believed it, and I believe it, too."

"She was right," Omari replied. "I'll make sure you will welcome her as you are now when she returns."

Nourbese looked at him with an expression conveying emotions beyond her age.

"Mama is not coming back," she said. "That is why I'm so sad. "I will miss her for the rest of my life."

"You don't know this," Omari said. "Your mama is a great warrior."

Nourbese tilted her head. "Can you promise she will return?"

Omari lowered his head. "No. I can't."

"Then it is done," Nourbese replied. She wiped the tears from her face with her sleeve. "I'm hungry. What did you bring us?"

Nourbese's changing the subject caught Omari off guard. His mind returned to the day his parents died. He had no one to take care of him. All he had was his wits. He allowed himself one day to grieve, then he went about creating his new life. It had been that way since. As he focused on Nourbese, he smiled. At least she had Eda. At least she had him.

"I caught a few stingers at the dock," Omari said. "They are small and full of bones, but they are tasty." He held up the stringer of fish and Nourbese studied them like a jaded market merchant.

"They are small," she finally said. "I hope they are filling."

"We're about to find out," Omari said, grinning.

He set about cooking the fish. The house was soon filled with the smell of roasting stinger fish. Omari hummed again, and Nourbese joined him, eventually complementing his voice. Omari found serving bowls in the pantry and filled them with the warm fish. They ate eagerly. Omari was sure he swallowed more than a few bones, but he didn't care. The fish was delicious. Nourbese sat beside him as she ate, complementing each bite with a hum. The fish was gone too quickly, but they were both full. The day's labor caught up with Omari, so he prepared a place to sleep. No sooner had he settled in did Nourbese join him, pressing against him. Omari smiled then drifted to sleep.

Nourbese was still beside him when he woke the next morning, snoring like an old drunk man. Omari chuckled as he eased away, making sure he didn't wake her. He donned his weapons then went to the dhow. After a quick inspection, he returned to the cabin and woke Nourbese. She rubbed her eyes then looked at him, a smile gracing her face.

"Good morning, Baba," she said.

"Good morning. It's time for us to leave. Gather your things."

They packed their belongings and ambled to the dhow. Omari lifted Nourbese and put her inside. He untied the mooring, gave the dhow a good push then jumped inside. He unfurled the sails and they were on their way. The winds were merciful, pushing the small craft out into the open sea. Omari was not a good navigator, so he kept the boat within sight of the shore. Nourbese leaned on the bulwark.

"I've never been on a boat before," she said. "This is beautiful."

"It is," Omari replied. "The sea can be temperamental. She is showing her best side today."

Nourbese looked at him. "She?"

Omari nodded. "Sati Baa gives life. So many depend on her bounty. The merchants and fishers make their offerings daily in praise and fear."

"Why would they fear her?"

"Sati Baa can be as dangerous as she is benevolent," Omari said. "The rainy season brings storms, and there is nothing like being caught in a tempest on the sea."

"Have you been in one?" Nourbese asked.

"A few times," Omari said. "Too many times."

"I would like to be in a storm," Nourbese said. "I would like to feel her strength."

"That's an odd thing for a child to say," Omari said.

"Is it?"

"Actually, I don't know. I haven't been around children since . . . since I was a child."

Nourbese followed him like a little shadow, helping when she could. They cast lines and caught a few fish to eat along the way, the best a large spinfish. Omari guided the dhow to the shore where he built a small fire and cooked their catch. The spinfish was especially pleasing.

They remained on the shore during the night, Omari telling stories of his life in Sat-Baa as a boy. When he was done, Nourbese was silent.

"Is something wrong?" he asked.

"Your life was very sad," she said.

Omari shrugged. "It was what it was. I never thought about it being happy or sad. I did what I had to do to survive. We all did."

"Mama raised me alone," Nourbese said. "When she discovered the ngisimaugi on my back, she said I could never let anyone know about it."

"Then how did the Ngola find out?" Omari asked.

"Emotan, the Ngola's sonchai," Nourbese replied. "She came to our home one day with the Ngola's guards. She said she sensed me, and her divination led her to us. She said I was destined for great things at the Ngola's side. But mama said no. When Emotan ordered the guards to take me, Mama drew her machetes." Tears formed in Nourbese's eyes and she pushed them away with her palms. "Emotan told them to kill Mama. I . . . I shouted no, then thrust my hands out. Something happened."

Omari leaned close to Nourbese. "What?"

"Emotan flew into the air then hit the ground. The guards ran to her. They called her name and shook her, but she did not move. Before they could look up, Mama killed them. We packed as much as we could, and we ran away."

"Your mama did the right thing," Omari said. "The Ngola was sure to kill her, then make you her new sonchai. But it seems Eda has other plans for you."

"Why must everyone have plans for me!" Nourbese slammed her fist into the dirt. "I just want to be with mama. I don't want to be a sonchai or a warrior!"

Omari put his hand on her small shoulder. "There are some things we don't get to choose. We have to make the best of them. It's all we can do."

He stood and gathered their things. "We'll camp away from the shore. The last thing I want to do is be a mamba's meal."

"I don't think you'd taste very good," Nourbese replied. "You look tough."

"I bet you taste like spinfish," Omari said.

They retreated into the bush a few strides until Omari found a suitable space. He prepared a space for them to sleep.

"Let's get some rest. We have a full day of sailing ahead, and you're going to help."

Nourbese clapped her hands then hugged him. Omari hugged her back and smiled.

"Okay, to bed with you."

Nourbese laid down on the leaves and straw he'd gathered and fell to sleep quickly. Omari sat up an hour longer, watching the fire slowly die as he contemplated his situation. All he wanted to do was go back to Sati-Baa and live a normal life. Well, as normal as life could be for him. He hoped this was his last obligation to Eda, that she would set him free to be his own man again. His eyes drifted to Nourbese. When he first saw her, he felt no obligation to her. The ways of Oyo were clear and he knew she was safe with Izegbe and Eda. But the weeks on the road had transformed those feelings. It would be hard to leave her with Eda, even though he knew she would be in the best hands.

Omari yawned and stretched. It was like he told Nourbese earlier; there are some things we don't get to choose. He went to his place and lay on his back. Sleep took him quickly.

*   *   *

Omari and Nourbese woke with the sunrise. They finished the fish for breakfast and began gathering their items. Omari was folding his blanket when he noticed smoke rising from the direction of the lake. He dropped his blanket, armed himself and began loading his hand cannon. Nourbese needed no words; she ran and took refuge behind him. Omari gave her a dagger and a club. Nourbese looked at him and Omari saw Izegbe in her expression. He winked and grinned.

Moments later Omari heard footfalls and voices. He raised the hand cannon and waited. As the strangers came into view, Omari lit the fuse. The hand cannon fired as their attackers entered the clearing. He dropped the weapon, pulled out his sword and dagger, and rushed through the smoke, striking down the screaming wounded men then killing the men behind them. He shuffled backwards then turned to run, grabbing Nourbese and plunging deeper into the bush. The others pursued them, the sound of breaking branches, and curses at their backs. Omari reached the thickest part of the bush then stopped.

"Keep running," Omari said. Nourbese nodded then disappeared.

Omari turned back. He used the foliage to his advantage, ambushing them one by one. He did not recognize these warriors; their clothing was different than any he's encountered in his travels. They fought fiercely, but their skills did not match his fury and determination. He soon found himself standing alone surrounded by the dead and dying.

"All that for nothing," someone growled.

A large man wearing a conical metal helmet and breast armor covered with talisman pushed through the brush, holding Nourbese by the neck. Omari had fought a man armored the same way in Kamit. Someone was hunting him.

"Let her go," Omari said. "I know why you're here."

The man bared his teeth then tossed Nourbese aside. Omari winced when she struck the ground. The man stepped forward, gripping his massive sword with both hands.

"Every day you live is an insult to Daarila," the man hissed.

"Then do something about it . . . if you can," Omari replied.

The men clashed. As soon as their swords met Omari knew he was in trouble. His would be assassin fought with skill and power, driving Omari back with every stroke. Omari dodged and ducked, fighting with pure instinct. The assassin's sword sliced his torso, blood staining his tunic. He blocked a stab at his neck and retaliated by slamming his blade against the assassin's helmet, knocking it from his head. The man staggered back, blinking his eyes clear of the blood running into them from the head wound. He ran toward the helmet; Omari threw his dagger, striking the man in the back of the neck. The assassin collapsed face first onto the ground, his body convulsing. Omari walked up to him, bruised, wounded, and exhausted. He stood over the dying man, raising his sword to deliver a killing blow.

Pain burst through his back and Omari yelled. He looked down to see a sword emerge through his stomach. The blade struck three more times before Omari fell to his knees and tumbled to his side. He rolled onto his back to see a man clothed like the one he'd just killed looming over him.

"Daarila's will be done," the man said.

The man raised his sword then yelled as his knee shattered. Omari saw Nourbese pounce on his shoulder, driving her dagger into his neck and head as they fell out of his vision. His back burned as his ngisimaugi fought to heal him, but it was too much. His thoughts went back to that day he lay dying in Wadantu; the day Eda saved his life. It was not to be this time. He could not feel Eda; he could only feel his body warmth fading as his eyesight dimmed. Nourbese appeared over him, tears in her eyes.

"I won't let you leave me!" she shouted.

She pressed her bloody hands on his wounds and Omari felt a surge of warmth. The power from his healing tattoo merged with whatever Nourbese triggered and the girl jerked. His body mended, but Omari saw the effect it was having on Nourbese.

"Stop," he whispered. "Let me go."

"No!" she shouted back. "You are my baba. You are all I have."

Another wave of energy swept through him, then another. Omari could feel his innards healing with each wave. Nourbese's face was blank, her eyes kipande blue. Omari's pain lessened and the warmth eased; Nourbese shared a weak smile then collapsed onto him. Omari strained to raise his arms then wrap them around his daughter. She still breathed but barely. He knew she would recover. He'd fought to protect her life, and she had saved him. It was then that Eda's visage appeared over them.

"Now you know," she said. "Bring our daughter home. You know the way."

Omari had so many questions, but fatigue overwhelmed him. He closed his eyes and embraced the peaceful darkness.

* * *

The sun's warmth woke Omari. Nourbese still lay on his chest, rising and falling with his breath. He held her as he sat up, frowning as his guts ached. Glancing down, he could barely see the scars from his wounds. It would take time to heal completely, but he would heal.

Nourbese stirred in his arms. "Baba? Are we dead?"

Omari squeezed her.

"Ouch!"

"No. We're not dead."

He let her go as he stood. The bodies of the assassins were gone. Whether it was scavengers or something more sinister, Omari didn't care.

"We have to go," he said. "Wadantu is not far."

"How?" Nourbese asked. "The bad men burned our dhow."

"Eda will provide," Omari said. He regretted his words as soon as he said them. He was sounding like a follower.

He gathered their weapons and secured them. He then took Nourbese's hand and they walked toward the lake.

"Thank you for saving my life," Omari said.

"Thank you for saving mine," Nourbese replied. "Mama and Eda would have been upset if you didn't."

"I couldn't let you die," Omari said. "You owe me an oware game."

Nourbese giggled. "You're silly, baba." She hugged his waist. "I love you."

Omari stumbled.

"Baba! Are you okay?"

Omari held Nourbese tighter. "Yes. I've never been better. I love you, too."

They reached the lakeshore. The remains of their dhow still smoldered, but nearby was the assassin's craft. It was a type of ship Omari wasn't familiar with, but it basically functioned the same way. Inside there were plenty of provisions and a map leading to Wadantu. A moderate breeze teased the sails.

"The winds blow in our favor. Let's take advantage of it," Omari said. They climbed inside; Omari raised the anchor, lowered the sail, and they set off. The winds blessed them for the next three days. On the fourth day the shores of Wadantu beaconed them. Omari guided the dhow close to the shoreline then gave the rudder over to Nourbese.

"Hold it steady," he said.

Nourbese nodded, her serious expression making him chuckle. He grabbed the mooring rope then jumped overboard, swimming until his feet touched bottom. From there he pulled the dhow as close as he could until it touched lake bottom. He waded back to the boat and carried Nourbese to shore.

"How far do we have to walk?" she asked.

"Not far," Omari replied. "Can't you feel it?"

Nourbese closed her eyes. "Yes. I can."

"Then you lead the way."

Omari put her down. Nourbese let go of his hand and walked toward the dense forest. As she neared the trees and bushes parted, opening a path for them. Omari picked up his pace, anticipating who they would see once their journey ended. The flora continued to separate for them until they reached small clearing. In the center of the clearing stood Eda. The mix of emotions she set off in him was there as he gazed upon her, a tempest of worship and desire.

Eda knelt and opened her arms to Nourbese. The girl ran and jumped into them and Eda embraced her.

"Nourbese," Eda said.

"Mama Eda," Nourbese replied.

Omari stopped a distance away, admiring the two of them together. Eda looked at him and smiled.

"Well done," she said.

Omari nodded. "It's not like I had a choice."

Eda laughed and Omari felt endless joy. "As you have seen, your daughter is special. She possesses the best of you, Izegbe . . . and me. She will be safe here."

"Can I stay the night?" Omari asked with a wink.

Eda shook her head. "Only you would wish be with me in such a way."

Eda walked to Omari then placed her hand on his cheek. Omari almost collapsed with pleasure.

"Go home, Omari," she said. "Sati-Baa awaits."

Omari was overcome by darkness. When he opened his eyes, he was in his boat. He was surrounded by provisions, enough to get him to the nearest seaport. He reached up and placed his hand where Eda had touched him. It was still warm.

A strong breeze filled the sails, pushing at the boat. Omari lifted the anchor then turned the boat about.

"Home it is," he said aloud. He manned the sails, beginning the last leg of his journey to Sati-Baa.

A Proper Homecoming

The Kamba Claw vibrated from the raucous drumming of the visiting musicians and foot stomping patrons. Brightly dressed servers weaved between dancers and tables, skillfully carrying food and drink to the celebrants. The serving house was experiencing a perfect storm; farmers rejoicing a good harvest, fisherfolk anticipating a spectacular snakefish season, and merchants eager to profit from trading the harvest and catch to eager customers beyond the lakeshore.

One of the servers worked her way to a table tucked in a corner opposite the entrance. A lone man sat there, his handsome face solemn despite the revelry around him. She'd watched him the entire night, hoping to get his attention beyond the food and beer he ordered. She imagined caressing his muscled arms, her legs wrapped around his hips as they pleasured each other over and over again. He looked into her eyes as she placed the plate of steamed shellfish and lakeweed before him then refilled his gourd with beer. His smile was like a ray of sun, yet his eyes remained restrained.

"Asante," he said in Tradespeak, his smooth deep voice stirring her.

"Is there anything else you desire?" she said. The man smirked and for a moment there was warmth in his eyes.

"I'm satisfied . . . for now," he replied. The man took more than enough cowries from his pouch and put them in the woman's hands. She grasped his wrist with her free hand.

"My name is Amkhitha."

"I'm Omari. Omari Ket."

"I am here for you, Omari Ket. For whatever you desire."

Omari smiled. "I'll remember that."

Amkhitha put the cowries in the collection pouch that hung from her hip. She strolled away, glancing over her shoulder and sharing a smile before getting back to work.

Omari watched Amkhitha leave, enjoying the extra sway of her hips that was meant for him. In other circumstances he would be anticipating the pleasures to come, but not this night. His normal carefree attitude escaped him. It had been this way ever since he left Wadantu. He played with his lakeweed while swirling his beer. Suddenly life had become serious, and he was not sure what to do. His daughter Nourbese lived in Eda's forest; her mother Izegbe disappeared into the chaos of war. He'd once again come close to death, saved by Nourbese's power. And assassins constantly sought him, determined to take his life in Daarila's name, for what he did not know. It would have been better if Eda had let him die the first time. He did not ask for any of this.

He finished his meal and drank his beer. The tavern customers continued to celebrate, their joviality irritating him. How could they be so happy when death mingled among them, waiting for the time to strike? He needed more beer.

"Amkhitha!" he shouted.

The server came almost immediately with beer. She filled his gourd then sat beside him, her face close.

"Are you sure there is nothing else you need?"

Omari tried to muster up the lust Amkhitha sought but he couldn't.

"No," he croaked.

Amkhitha glared at him as she stood. "A waste of my time!" She stomped away. Omari nodded in silent agreement.

The tavern door opened and a new group of customers entered.

"Ride the tide!" they shouted.

Omari's head jerked up at the sound of the familiar phrase. It had been years since he heard it.

"And raise the oars!" he shouted back.

He locked eyes with the group and they pushed their way to him. Omari stood to shake their hands, hug them, and beat their backs with his fists. The three men and two women filled the chairs at his table.

"Saatibaans!" Omari said. "You are the last people I expected to see here!"

A broad woman with long braids and a small smile smacked his shoulder. "And why is that? We go where the winds blow, and rumor is there's cowries and stacks to be made here."

A slim man with a scarred face and curious eyes stared hard at Omari.

"You look familiar," the man said. "What's your name?"

"Omari Ket."

The man jumped out of his seat and stumbled backwards. "Daarila's balls! It can't be!"

The others looked at him while Omari grinned.

"Should we know him?" the woman asked.

"Not unless you were a street rat," the man said. He turned his attention back to Omari. "I doubt you would remember me. I was boy when you . . . well, apparently you didn't die as the rumors said. I ran with the Nyumbu. I remember the day you beat up our entire gang. You took pity on me and tossed me into a trash pile instead of bashing my head in."

Omari chuckled. "I remember. You weren't very good fighters."

"Well now," the woman said. "Never met a street rat I didn't like. I'm Naya and this is my crew. The boy you threw in the trash is Khari. That's Zahara." She pointed at the tall woman with the bald head and crooked smile. "That big oaf is Baraka, and the fool that's drooling over the dancers is Amri. He'll be dancing and singing with them before the night is done, if he doesn't start a fight first."

Baraka was tall and round, as if an artist had drawn him with circles. He looked soft, but Omari could see the strength underneath his fat. Amri bounced in his chair, clapping his hand in time with the drummers. Omari had met a few people like Amri, people that could be as dangerous as they were lighthearted. His eyes lingered on Zahara. She had a plain looking face, but her muscled yet shapely body intrigued him.

Omari's melancholy evaporated in the presence of his home people. He waved Amkhitha over to the table.

"Drinks for my new friends," he said.

"As much as I love beer, I'd like to eat first," Naya said. "We've just landed and we're starving."

"Bring them whatever they want," Omari said. "I'll pay."

Naya's eyebrows rose. "Well now! Not only is he not dead, but he also seems to be a man of means."

"I have enough for you mahamaria," Omari said with a wink. Naya and her crew looked at Omari with suspicion. Omari nonchalantly sipped his beer.

"I know mahamaria when I see them," he said. "I've fought quite a few."

Naya folded her arms across her chest. "Where?"

Omari winked at Naya then looked to Khari. "You wondered what happened to me, Khari? I guess you heard I became the consort of a wealthy woman."

"I did," Khari replied.

"So I guess you also heard that I was accused of 'inappropriate' behavior with said woman."

"I did."

Omari sipped his beer. "It was a lie. But what was my word against a respected Sati-Baa merchant? I was tried and sentenced to death. However, my patron reconsidered. Instead, I was sold to the Kiswalans to become a Mikijen. So you could say she profited from my services in more ways than one. Some say it was the same as a death sentence. But it wasn't for me."

"You're lying," Baraka said.

Omari stood then lifted his shirt up to his chest. He turned, revealing his ngisimaugi.

"Damn it to the Cleave! It's true!" Amri exclaimed. "But . . ."

"Yes, I'm no longer a Mikijen, and yes, the ngisimaugi remains. Why, I don't know. Some say it's because I'm Eda blessed."

His new friends looked at each other then burst out laughing. Omari laughed with them. He didn't care if they believed him or not. Their presence was just what he needed to lift him out of his dark mood. He began rolling his shirt down.

"Can you leave it up a little longer?" Zahara said. "My eyesight isn't that good."

Omari took off his shirt and flexed. He was feeling better by the second.

Amkhitha and the other servers arrived with the food. Amkhitha froze for a moment, admiring Omari's naked torso. Naya took the tray from her hands and passed the food to everyone. Omari sat and drank more beer, winking at the supple server. He was settling into his chair when there was commotion coming from the floor. Naya looked up from her food and scanned the table.

"Where's Amri?"

Omari looked to the disturbance. "Over there."

He stood and began walking toward the ruckus. Amri was in a fighting stance surrounded by the musicians, with a wicked smile on his face. The musicians glared at him and waved their orinkas while the dancers hid behind them.

"What's the problem?" Omari asked.

One of the musicians stabbed a finger at Amri.

"Him! He ruined our performance with his terrible dancing!"

Amri huffed. "You must be mistaken. My dancing is admired throughout Sati-Baa!"

The musician rolled his eyes. "Then everyone in Sati-Baa must be as drunk as you!"

Amri made a move toward the man and the musicians swarmed him like angry hornets. Omari jumped in to pull Amri free and was hit hard by an orinka on the jaw. He answered the club blow with a kick that sent a man flying onto the stage and into the dancers.

"Ride the tide!" Omari heard Naya shout.

"And raise the oars!" the mahamaria answered as they rushed to the fight.

"And raise the oars!" Omari repeated. He grinned as he lifted a hapless musician over his head then slammed him on the floor. Now this was more like it.

* * *

Three bodies lay tangled on a wide mattress, all naked and glistening with sweat. Omari, the one of the bottom, stirred first. He attempted to sit up, but his companions were heavy and he was still drunk. Amkhitha, the person on top of him,

105

mistook his intentions. She moaned and push her hips against him.

"Stop, please," Omari said. "I'm hungry."

The third person rolled off Amkhitha and climbed out of the bed. Zahara searched the floor for her clothes and Omari watched. She wasn't as skinny as he thought.

"Get your eyes off my ass," Zahara said. "The little one wants your attention. I've had enough of the both of you."

Omari sat up, Amkhitha clinging to his neck. "Sounds like you didn't enjoy the night?"

Zahara looked at him as she put on her pants. "Oh, I enjoyed it. But not as much as you two did. You're welcome."

Omari laughed as Amkhitha frowned.

"I need your full attention, Mikijen," she said.

Zahara put on her shirt and shrugged. "What else do you have to do?"

Omari nodded. "We'll be down . . . eventually."

Zahara laughed as she left the room and closed the door.

Omari and Amkhitha joined the mahamaria later that morning, ambling to the table where the others sat enjoying a meal of sorghum, goat, and beer. Naya saw them and made room. The others nodded, and Zahara gave him a knowing grin.

Amkhitha kissed Omari's cheek and winked at Zahara. "I must go. Will I see you again?"

"I don't know," Omari replied.

Amkhitha kissed his mouth then strolled away.

"Looks like everyone had a good night," Naya said.

"I can't complain," Omari replied.

"I like how you handle yourself, Ket," Naya said. "I'm always looking for another crew member. Join us. The pay is shit but it's always exciting."

Omari shook his head. "Thank you, but no. I have other plans."

Zahara sipped her beer. "A person wearing a Wabenka anklet doesn't need money."

Omari cursed himself for being so absent minded. He glared at Zahara and she shrugged.

"I couldn't help but notice," she said. "It was the only thing you wore most of the night."

The mood at the table shifted. He was sitting among ma-hamaria he'd met the night before. Even if he'd known them for weeks, it didn't mean they wouldn't try to take advantage of the situation. It was like a starving man finding a stuffed and seasoned goat and trying to decide to eat it. He could run for the door and hope there were constables that would help him. He wore his jambiya; he could probably kill them all, but it wouldn't be easy. They were skilled fighters, and it would be sad having to do it, especially Zahara. There was a third option.

"I took a job with Kamit merchants which paid very well," he said. "It was too much for me to carry, so I deposited in a Wabenka bank."

"How much?" Khari asked.

"That's not important," Omari replied. "What is important is that I'm looking for a dhow to take me to Sati-Baa. I'll pay handsomely for it."

"And why should we accept payment when the only thing between us and a fortune is this table and a little bit of ankle bone?" Naya asked.

"If you know what a Wabenka bracelet is, you know how it works," Omari answered. "The bracelet will only be accepted if I present it."

"I know a few skilled sonchai in Sati-Baa," Baraka said. "All they would need is a lock of your hair, or maybe a bit of your blood."

Omari sighed. This wasn't looking good. His right hand went to his jambiya hilt. "We had such fun last night. I would hate to have to kill you all over a few stacks."

The mahamaria laughed.

"Calm down, rafiki," Naya said. "We have no intention of robbing you. We bonded last night, in more ways than one. We'd be happy to take you to Sati-Baa if we could."

"And why can't you?"

For the first time since Omari met Naya, she looked uncom-fortable.

"Certain circumstances requires that we stay away from the city for at least a few weeks."

"I guess I'll have to find someone else to take me," Omari said.

"What's your hurry?" Naya asked. "It will only be a few weeks."

"I've been away from Sati-Baa for ten years," Omari said. "I've walked every inch of Ki Khanga and never felt truly home. Now I have the means not only to return but establish something of my own. The closer I get, the more eager I am to see it done."

"Sati-Baa is not like you remember," Khari said. "It's changed, mostly for the worst."

"It can't be that bad," Omari said.

"It can," Khari replied. "The current Grand Merchant, Bunama Ogunsola, rules the city like he owns it. The constables serve him and function as his enforcers. He taxes everyone and everything, and the other merchants are so afraid of him that many have left the city."

"To go where?" Omari asked.

"The Middle Islands," Naya answered. "That's where we live. Sometimes. We can take you to Sati-Baa, but we would suggest you collect your stacks then move on. I don't know how much you have, but if it's a lot, it won't go unnoticed. Ogunsola has eyes everywhere."

This was not what Omari wanted to hear. He dreamed of owning a small tavern and a couple of fishing dhows. He would serve the best spinfish in all Ki Khanga and bore his patrons with his lies. What he knew of the Middle Islands was not good. It was a barren rock where dhows dumped their trash from the open lake before sailing to Sati-Baa

"I'll take my chances in Sati-Baa," he finally said.

"It's your stacks," Naya said. "Like I said, we have business to handle here. As soon as it's complete, we'll be happy to take you as far as the Islands. From there, you're on your own."

"Fair enough," Omari said. "Can I ask what your business is?"

"The dhow we sail isn't exactly ours," Naya said. "Although they say possession is nine tenths of ownership. We have an interested buyer; we're just waiting for the rest of the stacks."

"I will wait then," Omari said. Omari and Naya shook hands.

Naya leaned back in her chair. "Since we have decided to become partners, it sure would be nice to stay in town instead of on the dhow."

"Anything I pay for now comes out of your pay to get me to the Middle Islands."

Naya looked to the others. "What do you say?"

"I'd much rather stay here than on that boat," Baraka said. "It smells like fish, ass and sorrow."

"I vote for the tavern," Zahara said. "The company's better." She winked at Omari.

Khari nodded his approval and Omari smiled. He'd sold the assassin's dhow a few days ago. The cowries would cover the cost of their stay and leave a lot left over, which meant he wouldn't have to dip into his stacks. Once they reached the Islands, he'd have to check out the situation in Sati-Baa himself. It was the only way to be sure.

Omari secured the rooms for the mahamaria and they left the serving house for the docks. Omari walked with Naya, the others following.

"Who are we looking for?" he asked.

"I'll know her when I see her," Naya replied.

"You've done business before?"

"Many times. She's an honest person and pays well."

They walked a few more minutes before reaching a dock with three dhows flying a checkered banner.

"This is it," Naya said.

No sooner had the words escaped her lips did a dozen armed men leave the dhows and march toward them, their swords drawn. Omari's hands went to his blades but Naya shook her head.

"It's a show of force," Naya said. "They know who I am. They're just being assholes."

The first person to reach them was a dark brown skinned man with a weathered face and a beard that reached his belly. His dingy white long sleeved shirt jostled with talisman, his baggy leather pants flopping on his sandals. He confronted Naya with a sneer.

"State your business," he said with a piercing voice.

Naya rolled her eyes. "Must we go through this every time, Maumadu?"

Maumadu didn't reply.

"Maysa!" Naya shouted. "Call off your dog!"

Maumadu stepped forward, grasping his sword hilt. "You dare . . ."

Omari and the others surged forward. Omari's sword was already drawn, the tip at Maumadu's throat.

"Maumadu! Stand down!"

A tall woman dressed in the local finery strode down the plank of the nearest dhow; her wide eyes focused on Omari. Maumadu's companions made way for her.

"That's enough, Maumadu," she said.

Maumadu did not budge. "Maysa, you know how I feel about mahamaria."

"I know. But you know Naya. She's done nothing to you. Go back to the dhow."

"I can't leave you with . . ."

"Listen to your master," Omari said. He pressed the tip of his sword on Maumadu's neck, drawing blood. Maumadu's eyes flooded with fury.

"You and I will meet again," he said. "And when we do, you'll be the one who bleeds!"

Maumadu spun around them marched away. Maysa watched him and the others for a moment before turning her attention back to Naya.

"I told you to wait at the serving house," she said.

"Our circumstances have changed," Naya replied. "I have a new employer, so I must finish our business now."

"Who, him?" Maysa motioned her head toward Omari.

"Yes."

"And who are you?"

"Om . . . a person of means," Omari said.

"That doesn't tell me anything."

"It's all you need to know."

Maysa waved Omari off "Naya, where's my dhow?"

"Where's my payment? You promised half."

Maysa tossed back her robe, revealing a finely made leather bag hanging from her slim shoulder. Omari got a good look at

110

her and regretted being rude. Maysa took a hefty pouch from the bag and tossed it to Naya. Naya opened it then smiled. She closed the pouch and handed it to Zahara.

"Come," she said. "Your dhow awaits."

"Chomba! Ndemi! Come with me," Maysa called out.

The guards hurried down the plank to the deck. Maumadu followed them.

"I did not ask for you," Maysa said to Maumadu.

"I don't trust them," Maumadu replied.

"You've caused enough trouble, husband. Stay here and tend to things. This won't take long."

Maumadu glared at Omari before stomping away. Omari smiled.

"Let's go," Maysa said.

They trekked from the docks. Maysa made her way to Omari.

"You should take my husband's threat seriously," she said. "He's a dangerous man."

"I'll take your word for it," he said. "But you're husband knows nothing about me. Maybe he's the one who should be wary."

"Omari is a former Mikijen," Naya said.

Maysa's eyes went wide with fear. "Why didn't you say something?"

"I usually don't need to."

"I apologize for my husband," Maysa said. "He has bad history with Naya. Please do not kill him."

"I don't expect to see your husband again," Omari said. "Besides, I'm not a murderer. Well, not deliberately."

"I can pay you."

Omari tilted his head. "How much?"

"Two stacks."

"I'll consider it."

"Three."

"That sounds reasonable."

"I thank you."

Omari nodded, doing his best not to laugh. Naya looked and him then shook her head.

The road they followed turned into a wooded path as they left the port city. Minutes later they emerged into a clearing, a small cove where the stolen vessel rested.

"Your dhow," Naya said.

Maysa and her guards waded into the shallow water then climbed aboard using the rope ladder hanging from the bulwark. Naya, Omari, and the others waited on shore as they inspected their prize.

"Why did you take that woman's money?" Naya asked.

"That's what a hamaria would do."

"Why not?" Omari replied. "I'm paying for your rooms. Doesn't hurt to make a little money back."

"You really should be worried about Maumadu," Naya said. "He's a good fighter, and he doesn't forget. No matter what Maysa said, he'll be coming for you."

"I don't expect to be here that long," Omari said. "I plan to leave in the morning. I assume you have another dhow?"

"We do."

"Then we should be on our way. Your business is done here, and I'm anxious to get to Sati-Baa."

"So you're giving the orders now?"

"I'm paying you, so yes, I am."

"I'm not sure if I like you, Omari Ket."

"That's only because you didn't spend last night with me," Omari replied. "I think Zahara would have a different opinion."

Naya laughed. "You're not my type. Besides, Zahara likes everybody. She's no judge of character."

Omari chuckled. "So are we leaving tomorrow?"

"Yes," Naya said. "Our dhow is in a fishing village a few miles east of here. We'll rest tonight then be on our way in the morning."

"The dhow is acceptable," Maysa called out from the deck. "We can sail it back to our dock. I will pay you there."

The guards lowered the gangplank and Omari and the others boarded the dhow. When they reached Maysa's dhow, Maumadu and the others were waiting on the docks. Maumadu's swords were drawn.

"Shit," Omari said. Naya scowled then glared at Maysa.

"You weren't going to pay me, were you?"

The mahamaria drew their blades. Maysa rushed to Omari, grabbing his arm.

"This was Maumadu's idea. Let me talk to him."

"It won't do any good," Naya said. "You know that."

Maysa glared at Naya before turning back to Omari.

"Please."

"I have no wish to fight him," Omari said. "But I don't relish the idea of dying, either."

Maysa's people moored the dhow. Maysa was the first off the ship. She hurried to Maumadu and they immediately began to argue. Omari and the mahamari filed off the dhow, their eyes on the duo. Maumadu spotted Omari and he shoved Maysa aside.

"Mikijen!" he shouted. "Let's finish this. Then we'll deal with the others."

Omari dropped his head.

"You tried," Naya said.

Omari sheathed his blades then sauntered toward Maumadu. He raised his hands.

"Look, Maumadu. We don't . . ."

Maumadu yelled and swung at Omari's neck. The man clearly had knowledge of a Mikijen's weakness. He knew decapitation was instant death. Omari leaned away from the swinging then sidestepped, opening Maumadu's right torso to a killing thrust. But Omari didn't take it. Instead, he stomped the Maumadu's back leg, driving the man to his knee. Omari punched the man on the side of his head and he collapsed onto his side.

Maumadu scrambled back to his feet and attacked again. He was a better than average fighter, but he was no match for Omari. Omari continued to dodge and feint, hoping Maumadu would wear himself out and give up. His nonchalance almost cost him a serious wound. Maumadu feinted for Omari's neck then drove his short sword for Omari's heart. Omari twisted, avoiding the thrust but receiving a serious slash across his chest.

"Enough of this!" Omari growled.

Omari jerked his sword free then hit Maumadu jaw with his sword hilt, shattering it. He swept Maumadu's feet from under him and the man smacked the ground on his chest, his weapons flying from his grip. Omari stepped on Maumadu's right arm, raised his sword, then severed his right hand.

The onlookers gasped. Maysa ran to Maumadu then covered him with her body.

"Send for a healer!" she screamed. She glared at Omari and he shrugged.

"I didn't kill him," Omari said, then walked away.

Naya walked up and knelt beside Maysa. "I need the rest of my stacks. You know, the ones you weren't going to pay."

The healer ran up to them, dropping to his knees and opening her bag. As she worked on Maumadu's wrist, Maysa stood then walked away to her dhow. She returned minutes later with the stacks, shoving the bag into Naya's chest.

"I never want to see you again," she hissed.

"You won't," Naya replied. She walked away, glancing back at Maysa's guards to make sure they weren't following. She gave the bag to Khari and they departed. Naya went to Omari.

"You might as well have killed him," she said.

Omari glanced at Naya. "Really? He still had his life and Maysa. If the healer is good, he'll survive. He won't threaten anyone again unless he learns to fight with his left hand. No, I think I did him a favor."

"At least we got our pay," Naya said. "I don't think we'll be doing business here again."

"You won't have to," Omari said. "I'm going to need some help with what I have in mind. Your crew seems to be good enough."

Naya laughed. "It seems the situation has changed. I offered you employment, and now you're offering it to me."

"You'll have to come to Sati-Baa with me," Omari said.

"And that's the problem," Naya said. "I'll warn you again, Omari. Do not got to Sati-Baa. It's nothing like you remember."

"I have to see for myself," Omari replied. "Ever since my exile, I've dreamed of returning home. I have to go."

"At least go to the Middle Islands first. You can sail from there to Sati-Baa and collect your stacks. If you're lucky, you'll make it out with all of it."

"We'll see," Omari said.

The mahamaria returned to the serving house for their items. Amkhitha followed Omari outside, giving him a generous kiss goodbye. The trek to the next town took the remainder of the day; it was dark when they reached the serving house. The building was larger than the one they left behind, a two story structure with rooms to rent on the second floor. Omari secured their spaces, taking the largest room in the corner of the building with a view of the harbor. They ate a hearty meal of tigerfish, goat, and chicken, then washed it down with gourds of sweet beer. As they separated to go to their rooms, Omari noticed Zahara following him.

"It will just be the two of us," he said.

"I prefer that," Zahara replied. "That means I don't have to share." Zahara reached into her bag and took out a large pouch of chagga. Omari's grin became a wide smile.

The night was much better with just the two of them. They slept for a time, then Omari awoke. He took his pipe from his bag and stuffed the bowl with Zahara's chagga. He lit the bowl with his flint and moments later the savory aroma of the weed filled the room. Omari took a long drag then moaned.

"This is good," he whispered.

"It is?"

Zahara sauntered to him then took the pipe from him. She took a drag, closed her eyes as she inhaled, then smiled. "It is."

Omari sat on the windowsill and Zahara joined him. They were silent for a time, letting the chagga take effect while admiring the moonlight rippling over the calm waters. A mild breeze blew in from the lake, chilling their bare skin.

"So, how did you end up with Naya?" Omari asked.

"Kinda like you," she replied. "We met in a serving house and we hit it off. There was a fight, and I was part of the crew."

"And before then?"

"This and that. I traveled about the lake working when I needed to and doing other things when I had to. Naya is a good nahoda, so I stuck around."

Omari took another drag. "So where is home?"

"Fez."

Omari studied Zahara for a moment then smiled. "I can see it in your eyes."

"You've been to Fez?"

"I've been everywhere. You're a long way from home."

"That's on purpose. I come from a family of sangomas. I didn't want to be one, so I left."

"You haven't been working your ashé on me, have you?"

"That's natural."

Zahara took another pull on the pipe. "I never began training, but there are some talents that come naturally. I'm sensitive to those with strong ashé. People like you."

"I guess that's my ngisimaugi. It contains kipande."

"It's not just that," Zahara replied. "There's something more. It's raw, but it's there." Zahara touched the faint scar on his chest. Ten years ago it was a jagged tear; now it seemed no more than a birth mark.

"Here," she said. "What happened?"

"I died," Omari said, "and Eda saved me."

Zahara sat up straight, her eyes wide. "You're lying."

Omari shook his head. "Why would you say that when you sensed it? I was with a group seeking something of value in Wadantu. We were attacked, and I suffered a mortal wound to my heart. Eda healed me and sent me on my way."

"Why?" Zahara asked.

"I don't know," Omari replied. "I think there is something I must do. Nothing has been revealed to me, and honestly, I hope it never is. Sometimes I wish I'd been left to die."

"You don't mean that," Zahara said.

"No, I don't," Omari confessed. "But it sounds good to say. Like I have some control over what's going on."

"You should be thankful that Eda watches over you. There are some that would sacrifice everything for it."

"I'm not one of them," Omari replied. "Let me be to live my life as I wish. That is all I've ever wanted." Omari took puff. "Why am I talking to you about this?"

"Because of the chagga, and because I'm a good listener," Zahara said. She took the pipe from his hand and emptied the contents into a stone tray. "But we've talked enough. This is a good high. Let's not waste it."

She stood, grasped his wrist, then pulled him toward the bed. Omari grinned as he followed.

* * *

Omari and the mahamaria had a leisurely morning before setting out for the Middle Islands. The winds were favorable so they crossed the distance quickly. After four days on the open sea the Middle Islands came into view. Omari, Naya, and Khalil stood at the bow, watching dark smoke rise from the mountainous landscape.

"Something's not right," Naya said. "That's not chimney smoke."

"A hamaria raid no doubt," Khalil said.

"A large one," Omari agreed.

"Or something worse," Naya said.

Omari looked at the worried nahoda. "Worse?"

Naya looked at him. "Bunama Ogunsola."

"The grand merchant? How? Sati-Baa is a merchant city. It has no army, let alone a navy."

"Ogunsola has the stacks to hire both, and he's long hated the growing rivalry with the Islands. I'd bet my legs this is his doing."

The evidence grew worse the closer they came. Burned out dhows and boats bobbed in the waters, covered with the bodies of their crews.

"Maybe we should go back," Zahara said.

"I agree," Omari said. "Whoever did this could still be on the island."

"I'm going ashore," Khari said.

"That wouldn't be wise," Omari warned.

"He has family on the island," Naya said. She placed a comforting hand on Khari's shoulder. "I'll go with him. The rest of you can stay on the dhow. We'll take the landing boat."

"You don't go without me," Zahara said.

"And me," Baraka.

"This is not smart," Omari advised.

"We are a crew," Naya said. "You can stay on the dhow, although it would be helpful to have you with us."

"I didn't come all this way to die on an island," Omari said.

"Like I said, you can stay on the dhow. And if things go wrong, you'll become the owner."

"Damn it to the Cleave!" Omari said.

Naya smiled. "I assume that's a yes?"

Omari folded his arms and pouted. "Let's just get this over with."

They sailed the dhow to the nearest dock. Zahara jumped out and secured the dhow and the others disembarked. The smell of death was strong; they covered their mouths and noses with cloth before searching the dock. Most of the bodies were of locals; as they entered the town bodies clothed in similar uniforms appeared among the townsfolk. This was where the townsfolk began to fight back, Omari surmised. He expected the mahamaria to seek out certain homes where their families lived, but instead they kept walking.

"I thought you had family here, Khari," he said.

"I do," Khari replied. His face was stern as he spoke. "They would have fled at the first signs of danger."

"Where to?"

"The mountain caves," he replied. "The islands are used to mahamaria attacks. Usually our flotilla is strong enough to turn them back. Most never reach the shores. If they do, the dock marines are very capable. This must have been a large attack." He pointed to the mountains. "When there is an attack, the harbor drums sound and the people evacuate to the mountains. They hide in the caverns until the drums call them back."

"By the looks of things, that never happened," Naya said. "The dead are either marines or people who came back to see if it was clear."

"There are only so many provisions in the caverns," Bakara said. "If they have been there for weeks, they could be starving."

"We should make sure there's no more attackers here before we go," Zahara said. "They could follow us to the caverns. Omari and I will stay here. You three can go to the caverns."

"I'd rather go to the caverns," Omari said.

118

Zahara shook her head. "You fight better than them."

"It's a good plan," Naya said. "Let's go."

They continued until they reached the opposite end of the town. Omari and Zahara stood watch as Naya, Khari, and Bakara disappeared into the dense forest, waiting another hour to make sure no one followed. Omari took the time to load his hand cannon and inspect his weapons.

"Where did you get that?" Zahara replied.

"In the east," Omari said. "There's a land known only to the Kiswala where they trade for exotic items. I was stuck there for a time."

"How does it work?"

"If we have any trouble, I'll show you."

"I hope you don't have to show me." Zakara looked up into the sky. "It's been long enough. Let's do a walkabout."

Omari followed Zahara through the empty streets. Omari's mood turned grim. He'd seen such scenes many times; in some cases he and his mercenary cohorts were the cause of it. It was one of the reasons why he yearned to return to Sati-Baa. He was weary. Fighting and stealing would become a part of his past. He would finally settle down.

They worked their way back to the docks, found a clear platform and sat, their feet dangling over the turgid water. Omari took out his chagga pipe and Zahara handed him her herb pouch.

"This doesn't make any sense," he said as he filled the pipe. "This hurts Sati-Baa, most of all the grand merchant."

"True," Zahara agreed. "But there are rumors that Ogunsola has found another source of wealth."

Omari lit the pipe. "Where? Sati-Baa reaches everywhere in Ki Khanga."

"The Cleave."

Omari laughed. "Nothing lives in the Cleave. Daarila took care of that."

He took a drag on the pipe then handed it to Zahara. She did the same, exhaling through her nostrils.

"If you believe that, you're a fool," she said. "The sonchai of Fez journey into the Cleave as a rite of passage. They return . . . different."

Omari gave Zahara a skeptical glance and she shoved him. "It's true! I've seen it in my own family. My brother Hazeez took the pilgrimage. We were close growing up, only a year apart. After completing his training he made the journey. When he returned, I barely recognized him. I remember that day. I rushed to greet him and he looked at me like I was nothing. It was not just me, but everyone. Not long after he went to the capital city. I never saw him again. That's when I decided to leave."

"Are you sure . . ."

"I'm positive," Zahara said. "As sure as I sit here with you."

Omari was about to take another pull from the pipe when he spotted a sail in the distance. "Someone's coming."

Omari put out the pipe and they retreated into an abandoned warehouse. It was a baghlah, a large dhow used for deep ocean merchant voyages. But this one was modified to carry warriors, not cargo. The Kiswala owned many such dhows, but this was the first time Omari had seen one on the Sait-Baa sea. As the dhow came closer, Zahara scowled.

"That's Ogunsola's banner. We should warn the others."

They left the ruins, running through the town and into the bush. They followed the trail the others took, eventually finding themselves at the base of a cluster of forest covered hills. Beyond the hills rose mountains, their snowcapped obscured by dense clouds The trail narrowed as they entered the hills, eventually disappearing.

"What now?" Omari asked.

"We must wait," Zahara replied. "We have no choice."

Omari thought about taking out his pipe again but decided not to. Instead he squatted behind a stout tree and took out his hand cannon.

"I'll keep an eye on the trail from the town," he said. "You can look out for the others."

Zahara nodded then continued into the hills. Omari sat then leaned against the street. He closed his eyes, imagining his return to Sati-Baa, collecting his stacks, and living the life he dreamed of as a rat running the alleyways. Aisha's face appeared and he smiled. He wondered what had become of her; if she was still surviving the best she could, or if she had found a wealthy person to provide her with the life she deserved. Maybe she learned a trade. Whatever the circumstances, he hoped she was free of suffering as well.

Rough voices and footfalls broke his musing. Omari picked up his hand cannon before peeking around his cover. Five men advanced up the trail, followed by a huge beast Omari had never seen before. The creature stopped and raised its massive head, its nostrils flaring. Whatever it was, it was following the scent trail. He and Zahara had led them to where the townspeople hid.

Omari considered his options. He could work his way around them, hoping he wouldn't be seen, heard, or smelled. He could find a smaller dhow and sail on to Sati-Baa alone. He had no allegiance to the people on the island or the mahamaria and he was still skeptical of what he was hearing of Ogunsola. No grand merchant had ever been so powerful; the unwritten rules of the city prevented it. He would find out for himself.

The beast bellowed and the men jumped out of its way. Omari's mind was made up for him; the beast was coming for him. He snatched up the hand cannon, forcing himself to wait until the beast was only a few strides away before lighting the fuse. The beast was only steps away when the cannon discharged, the iron pellets ripping the beast's face apart. Omari dodged to his left as the beast's momentum carried it into the tree where he hid. It cracked the tree then collapsed on its side.

Omari using its thrashing and the cannon's smoke as cover. He took out his sword and dagger, working his way around the commotion then attacking from the right. He took down the first three men before they knew what was happening: the fourth man putting up a decent fight before succumbing to a stab to the ribs. The fifth man fled. Omari chased him down, slashing his hamstrings from behind then stabbing him in the base of the neck.

He'd started the fight, now he had to finish it. He walked down the trail toward the town and was met by the sight of a dozen more men with swords and spears. Omari turned and ran, bypassing his grim handiwork and continuing into the hills.

"I hear them!" someone shouted. "This way!"

Ogunsola's men weren't the only ones that heard the fighting. Naya and the others came running down the hill with at least twenty armed townsfolk.

"They're coming!" he shouted. The others ran by and Omari joined them. The clash was brutal and swift. The townsfolk wasted no time killing their attackers. They continued into the town to the dhow, overrunning it before the crew had time to flee. They spared no one, mutilating the bodies beyond recognition. From what they'd suffered, Omari didn't blame them.

The townsfolk wandered away after the slaughter, speaking to each other as they drifted to their homes. Omari gathered with the other mahamaria.

"Doesn't look like they needed our help," Omari said.

"They didn't," Naya said. "All they needed was a little encouragement."

"We told them you were sent by the Kiswala to help them," Khari said. "And we convinced them to leave the island. We're sailing south as soon as we can gather their belongings and make a few dhows seaworthy. The Cluster Islands are smaller, but they are fertile and beyond Ogunsola's reach. At least for now."

"May Eda bless you," Omari said. "I'm going to Sati-Baa."

"Why?" Naya asked. "This is what waits for you there."

"I've dealt with people like Ogunsola before," Omari replied. "The Middle Islands were competition, so he eliminated them. It's a warning to anyone that would defy him, although it won't make a difference beyond the lake. I don't care what he's built, he's not ready to face the other nations of Ki Khanga. They're much better at making war."

Omari lit his chagga pipe again. "Besides, I have a fortune waiting for me." He walked to the docks, seeking a decent dhow.

"We'll take you," Naya said. "But we will not dock."

"That's good enough," Omari said.

"Let's get this over with then," Naya said.

They assisted the townsfolk in gathering what belongings they could salvage and loading them on the seaworthy dhows. Some of the fisherfolk rowed out to collect their boats that had drifted away. By nightfall they were ready to evacuate. The town elders decided they would wait until morning; they spent the evening placating the spirits of the dead and making libations to the ancestors and spirits for protection during their upcoming journey. Omari and the mahamaria set up their own camp near the docks. They feasted on food given to them in payment for helping the townspeople, then slept as soon as the sun escaped below the horizon.

The next morning they ate a quick breakfast before setting off for Sati-Baa. A clear sky ruled over the blue waters, the winds swirling as they always did over the northern sea. Navigating the unpredictable breezes took skill, and Naya's crew possessed them. Omari helped when he could, but it was clear that he was outmatched by the others. They sailed for three days, taking a brief respite on the second day at an uninhabited island that served as a rest stop for water and whatever wild game hunters could claim. Naya's crew did neither. They rested from the difficult route, Omari and Zahara stealing away to enjoy each other. Omari was growing to like Zahara more than he should. They were alike in many ways. If it wasn't for the fact they were on their way to Sati-Baa, he could see them travelling together. But his traveling days would soon be over, and there was no one he wanted to see more than Aisha. So he would enjoy whatever time they had then end things at the right time.

They set sail after their brief respite, fighting the precarious winds for another day. As the sun set on the third day, Sati-Baa came into view.

Omari had no idea how he would feel when he finally saw his home. Hundreds of dhows from different lands rose and fell on the gentle waves that lapped on the beaches and against docks. Two and three story merchant houses edged the shore, their whitewashed tabby stone walls and ochre ceramic roofs a welcome home banner to his watery eyes. Night crier voices drifted from the watchtowers across the distance, calling for the night torches to be lit and sharing blessings for a peaceful night. A rush of emotions hit him, fueled by a flood of memories both good and bad. He stood motionless on the bow, his hands gripping the bulwark so hard his fingernails threatened to crack. His brief memories of his family were overwhelmed by darker thoughts; the bacillus epidemic that claimed both his mama and baba; the years of hiding and starving in the streets and alleys before he grew into his own and became the person everyone feared; his quiet times and pleasures with Aisha, and his forced exile because of a jealous and powerful merchant. Those morbid musings melted away the closer they came to the docks. If he had any doubts of going ashore, they were swept aside by the sight before his longing eyes.

He felt someone beside him and turned his head to see Naya.

"It's still beautiful from a distance," she said.

"It is," Omari replied. "I can't wait to walk her streets again."

"The Jewel doesn't shine as bright as it used to. You'll see."

They sailed closer, encountering the hectic landing traffic. Dhows passed them, the crews sharing customary greetings that had existed for centuries. They reached the point where the cargo canoes met those dhows that did not wish to dock and preferred to transfer their goods. Naya went to her cabin then returned with a small conch shell hanging from her neck with a coral chain. She blew three times, repeating until she was answered. Minutes later a canoe came in their direction rowed by four lean, bare-chested me, their bronze skin darkened by unimpeded sunlight. Naya blew again so the boatmen could adjust their direction. They pulled alongside the dhow then climbed the nets that were lowered to them. The lead boatman, a short, broad man with a bald head and gray beard, approached Naya.

"You have cargo?" he asked.

"We have a passenger," Naya said.

The man frowned. "The price is the same. Ten cowries."

Naya's eyes went wide. "Ten cowries! That's ridiculous!"

Omari waited for the negotiations to begin, but they did not.

"Ten cowries are the price decreed by the Grand Merchant. We have no say in it," the cargo man said. "The tax is five cowries. The rest goes to us." There was anger in his voice, but not for Naya. The porters turned away and ambled to the nets.

"Ten cowries is a good price," Omari said. He stepped forward, opened his bag, and took out the cowries. The lead boatman smiled as he took them.

"Let's go," he said.

"Wait." Zahara came forward. "I'm going with you."

Omari eyebrows rose. "For what?"

"For the pay. You're going to need someone to show you around and watch your back."

Naya stepped between them. She was not happy.

"You're leaving us just like that?" she said to Zahara. "What about your obligation to the crew?"

"You don't own me," Zahara replied. "I've always gone my own way. You know that. So I'm getting on this boat with Omari."

Naya's expression hardened. "Be gone, then."

Zahara laughed. "I didn't say I was gone for good. Besides, Omari doesn't seem like the person who likes people to be around long."

"It depends on the person," Omari said. He grasped wrists with Naya. "Thank you for your help. My offer still stands. I could use someone like you once I get my serving house."

"We'll get our people settled, then we'll see," she answered. As Zahara climbed down the net, Naya pulled Omari close and whispered in his ear.

"Watch her," she said. "Zahara looks out for herself."

"We have that in common," Omari replied. "Don't worry about me, Naya. I'm Eda blessed."

Naya laughed. "So you say."

Omari followed Zahara down the net and into the boat. Once their gear was secure, the rowers pushed away from the dhow and rowed toward the docks. At first Omari sat, but the closer they came his anticipation overwhelmed his calmness. He stood, the smile on his face growing with each oar stroke. Familiar sounds and smells tantalized him. The chatter of fisherfolk, merchants, and dockworkers speaking trade tongue as only a Satibateen could was like a favorite song being heard again. As the boat reached the coral stone stairs to the dock platform, Omari felt a tear roll down his cheek.

"Are your crying?" Zahara asked.

"Yes," Omari replied. "Yes I am."

Omari and Zahara gathered their gear and climbed out of the canoe. The climb up the stairs felt like a victor's ascent, each step a confirmation of his return. He reached dock level then stood still, turning his head slowly from left to right, taking in the hustling people around him and the grandeur beyond them. He had returned to the greatest city in Ki Khanga, and there was no describing the joy he felt.

A warm sensation from the anklet drew his attention. He pulled up his pant leg; the metal pulsed with a faint bluish glow. Omari dropped his pant leg then smiled at Zahara.

"My fortune calls me," he said. "Let's go get it."

They entered the city. The press of the crowd, the cornucopia of smells from the merchant food stalls, and the cacophony of voices was better than any chagga he'd smoked. He walked the streets with the confidence of a person born to them, which he was. His view changed, his eyes searching and finding the shadow folks, those who eked a living by begging, stealing, or taking advantage of a kind or naïve soul. Memories rose to mind both good and bad, all swirling together to become the man that he was. But there was something different about the people he observed. A sense of darkness seemed to follow them. Their eyes darted about anxiously, and they jumped at sudden movements. The life of street folk always carried a level of fear. This felt like terror.

The increased pulsing of the anklet broke his musing. Omari looked to his right and saw the elaborate arch indicating the beginning of the merchant district. He was about to turn in that direction, but instead he veered left. Zahara tugged his sleeve.

"Where are you going?" she asked. "The Wabenka bank is that way."

"There's something I want to see first," he replied.

"More than collecting your fortune?"

"Yes."

They walked for another hour, the buildings and people becoming less distinctive as they progressed. Zahara grasped the hilt of her sword, her eyes darting about. This was northern Sati-Baa, a part of the city far from the prosperity of the docks and the merchants whose wealth came from the sea trade. The

126

livelihood of the inhabitants of this part of the city relied on the large farms to the north, vast tracks of fertile ground owned by hereditary landowners. Work was hard and pay was little, with some planters using family groups who lived on the land and served as indentured labor. Omari's life in the streets had taken a fateful turn because of one of them.

He finally reached his destination, a section of small dwellings crushed together and piled atop one another. The people moving among the unkempt streets were more relaxed and jovial than those of the city despite their lowly means. Some of them glanced at the two, their garb standing out among those with lesser means. It was a sign that they were outsiders, which could draw unwanted attention, but Omari didn't care. While the adults subdued their curiosity, the children did not. They stared, whispered, and laughed as they followed them. One boy was brave enough to tug on Omari's sleeve. Zahara waved him off.

"Go away," she growled.

"Leave him be," Omari replied. He reached into his pouch and took out a handful of cowries. The children crowded around him as he passed them out.

"Why did you do that?" Zahara asked. "They'll be back for more."

Omari didn't answer. Many years ago he was just like them. This was his life before the bacillus epidemic. He jumped at them and growled and the children ran away laughing. The adults saw his humor and relaxed.

Omari stopped before a group of buildings, staring at a unit in the center. Zahara moved closer to him.

"Was that your home?" she asked.

"Yes," Omari replied. "I'm surprised it's still standing."

Zahara looked about. "I don't see how you found it. They all looked the same."

"Not to me," he replied.

The present faded away, replaced by the ghosts of the past. Omari saw his mother sitting outside their door, scrubbing the clothes of their neighbors in a wooden barrel. People walked by and spoke, mostly sharing good words and friendly jibes. He played in the streets with the other children, stopping only

127

when his mama yelled at him to fetch another bucket of water from the community well. His baba would return at dusk with the other farm laborers, sometimes with extra sorghum or berries he managed to steal from the harvest. They would go inside and baba would start a small fire while mama prepared the only meal of the day. Omari would eat while mama and baba spoke about their day and shared the latest gossip. They had nothing to spare, but they rarely went without. Until the epidemic.

Omari walked up to the woman sitting before his former home, a solemn look on her worn brown face. She jumped to her feet when she noticed him, but it was too late for her to run. Omari raised his hands and bowed.

"I mean you no harm, aunt," he said, addressing her as he would an elder relative. Omari reached into his pouch and took out a handful of cowries.

"May Eda bless you," he said as he gave her the cowries. She gasped as she accepted them, then looked into Omari's eyes with gratitude.

"She has through you," the woman replied.

Omari bowed again then turned and walked away. Zahara hesitated before following him.

"That was generous of you," Zahara said. "I'm surprised we weren't attacked."

"One thing you learn in the streets is who's an easy target and who isn't. Those who don't are dead."

"Makes sense," Zahara replied. "I hope you kept enough cowries for me."

"I have enough for me," Omari replied. "Don't worry, you'll get yours. There will be more than enough when I collect from the Wabenka."

They worked their way back to the merchant district, arriving at the Wabenka compound just before dark. The gate guards confronted him as he expected, stern faces with raised spears. Omari lifted his pant leg, revealed the anklet and they let them through. The Sati-Baa compound was much grander that its southern counterpart, boasting a wide courtyard created with stone hewed from the nearby Cleave peaks. Gardens were spaced evenly along the pathway to the bank, with patrons and workers enjoying the waning sunlight. Steep stairs led to the entrance of the main building, its gilded, exquisitely carved mahogany doors flanked by more guards. Omari showed the anklet again and was allowed inside. Zahara was not.

"Only those with official business with the Wabenka are allowed inside," the burly guard informed them.

"She's my bodyguard," Omari replied. The guards were unmoved.

"I'm okay," Zahara said. "I'll wait in the courtyard."

The inside of the Wabenka bank was similar to the bank in Kamit. A lone woman with obsidian skin and braided hair sat at a large wooden desk, reading the large ledger before her. She wore the royal blue robe of a Wabenkan accountant, a necklace with a golden pendant around her narrow neck. She looked up at Omari, lowering her spectacles. She closed the tome then stood. She was tall and thin, similar to the cattle people native of northern Aux.

"How may I assist you?" she asked.

"I have come to collect a deposit," Omari replied.

"May I see your identification?"

Omari lifted his pant leg, revealing the anklet.

"One moment, please."

The woman walked away; she returned with a broad brown man wearing black pants and a light blue tunic. The man carried a short rod that casted a blue glow similar to the pulsing anklet. The man nodded then knelt, touching the rod to the anklet. Letters formed on the rod as the man stood.

"Omari Ket," the man said.

"That's me," Omari said with a smile.

The woman nodded to the man and he disappeared into the innards of the building.

"Follow me," the woman said. She led him to a room with a small table and three chairs. Two of the chairs rested behind the desk. The woman gestured to the single chair.

"Bwa Omari Ket, please wait here. I will return momentarily."

Omari settled into the chair. A few minutes passed before the accountant returned with a ledger accompanied by a man dressed in merchant garb signifying him as a member of one of the local guilds. The man looked at Omari as if he was disgusting.

"This ledger lists what is owed to you by the bank," the woman said. Omari took a look at the amount and did everything in his power to keep from whooping in joy. Instead he vigorously cleared his throat.

"That seem correct, although I'll have to have my counters confirm," he said.

The accountant nodded. "Due the decree established by Grand Merchant Ogunsola, your money is subject to the merchant tax."

Omari rolled his eyes. He gave up a good portion of his payment to the bank, now he had to give more.

"I am not a merchant," Omari argued. "The tax should not apply to me."

"Anyone possessing the amount you have is considered a merchant in the eyes of the council," the man sitting beside the account said.

"And who are you?" Omari asked.

"The grand merchant's tax collector assigned to this bank," the man replied.

"Another greedy mouth to fill," Omari said. "So how much is it?"

"Fifty percent," the man said.

Omari sprang to his feet, the chair flying against the wall. "Fifty percent! That's insane!"

"That is the law," the man said. "We will collect as soon as the transaction is fulfilled."

"Only if the transaction is fulfilled," the accountant corrected. Her expression revealed her distaste for the tax collector.

"To the Cleave to all of you!" Omari stomped out of the building and across the courtyard, ignoring Zahara. He was outside the compound and into the crowd before she caught him.

"What happened?" she asked.

"Nothing. Absolutely nothing!" Omari shouted.

He spotted a serving house and went inside, sitting at the first empty table he found. A server came to the table immediately.

"Spinfish and beer," Omari said.

The server looked to Zahara. "The same," she said.

"So did you get your stacks?" Zahara asked.

"No," Omari replied. "They want fifty percent."

Zahara whistled. "That's a lot. But you'd still be wealthy, won't you?"

Omari slammed his fist on the table. "That's not the point! The Wabenka already took their portion, and now this stupid grand merchant wants steal half of what's left!"

The patrons looked at Omari, their expressions showing their annoyance. The server brought their beers; Omari drained his before the server could leave.

"Another," he said.

"You have no choice," Zahara said. "That's the way it is now. Many are angry, but what can they do?"

"Well for one, the merchant council can vote for a new Grand Merchant," Omari replied. "I'm sure they're feeling the pinch, too."

"You weren't listening to Naya when she told you about Ogunsola," Zahara said.

"I was, but I didn't expect it to be this bad," he said.

"Yes, you did. You just didn't expect it to hurt you."

Omari finished his second beer. "I didn't."

"Ogunsola is a scourge to everyone. Prices are higher, wages are lower, and his constable forces terrorizes everyone."

"Then why hasn't anyone done anything about him?"

Zahara finished her beer then wiped her mouth with her sleeve. "Because they are afraid." She looked about the serving house. "Be careful what you say, and how loud you say it."

"Who needs so much wealth?" Omari continued.

"The greedy," Zahara replied. "Although some say Ogunsola's profits go beyond Sati-Baa."

"Where?" Omari asked.

"The Cleave."

"Daarila's balls! Not that again," Omari said.

Their meals arrived, spinfish fried whole with lake leaves, wild onions, and cliff goat. The presentation and aroma brought a smile to Omari's face despite his sour mood. He tasted each of them and nodded.

"At least the food is still as good as I remember. Another beer."

They ate in silence, the delicious meal calming Omari. But as soon as he swallowed the last piece of spinfish, his anger returned.

"I should just leave it all there," he said. "I never imagined having so much wealth, and when I think about it, I'd be just fine without it. I'm back home. I can make do."

"But you deserve it," Zahara said. "Let them have their share and be done with it."

"That's just it," Omari said. "It's not their share."

He searched the serving house until he saw their server and made eye contact.

"Another beer!"

"I'll be back," Zahara said. "I need to piss."

Omari drank two more beers and finished his meal before he realized Zahara hadn't returned.

"Where in the Cleave . . ."

A group of men entered the serving house. They scanned the patrons until their eyes fell on Omari.

"That's him!" one of them yelled.

Omari was already running to the back of the serving house. He stumbled through the prep space then outside to the kitchen. The workers all stood together, surrounded by more men with swords.

"Shit!"

Omari ran as the swordsmen joined the chase. Omari had a flashback of himself as a boy, fleeing the constables, but it didn't last long. Then he was running from punishment; now he was running for his life. He turned the corner and ran into a large man carrying a crate on his shoulders. Both fell, the man cursing on his way to the ground. Omari cursed back until the crate hit him on the head and knocked him cold.

* * *

Omari awoke in a soft bed, the mattress smelling of flower petals and spice. His head throbbed but the ngisimaugi flashed and the pain disappeared. He sat up to discover himself dressed new garments; the kind well-to-do merchants wore. The room he rested in was simple yet well-appointed with a chest of drawers, a nightstand, and a writing desk. If he had to guess, he was in the house of a merchant or someone else of means. The real question was whether he was there as a guest or a prisoner. At least he was alive.

His weapons were nowhere to be seen. He sat up then put on the sandals at the foot of the bed which fit perfectly. As he was standing, the door to the room opened and Zahara entered, a smile on her face.

"You're awake. Good."

And just like that Omari was angry again. His first instinct was to strangle Zahara to death. He was sure she was behind the attack at the serving house. But if he did, he'd have no idea what predicament he was in. So he scowled instead.

"You set me up."

"I did."

"You could have asked me to come with you."

Zahara shrugged. "I could have, but you ask too many question. I and my clients had no time for that. It was the only way I could get you here expeditiously."

"Where is here?"

"Come and I'll show you."

Omari followed Zahara out of the room and down a wide hallway. At the end of the corridor were two doors carved with Kiswala patterns, revealing to Omari that whoever owned this home was well traveled. Zahara opened the door, exposing a small meeting room. In the room sat six people, each wearing similar dark green robes. Omari smirked.

"The merchant's guild," he said.

"Yes," Zahara replied. She crossed the room and took a seat among them.

One of the merchants, a strikingly beautiful woman with a bald head and piercing amber eyes stood and acknowledged him.

"Welcome to our meeting, Omari Ket. I am Drucilla Okobe, second of the Merchant Guild. You honor us with your presence."

"It's not like I have a choice," Omari replied.

"You do," Drucilla said. "You can leave now. Zahara will guide you back to the city and we'll never see each other again. Or you can stay and listen to our proposal. I think you'll find it lucrative, and a solution to all of our problems."

"Which is?"

A servant entered the room as if on cue, carrying an ornate chair which he set down behind Omari. It seemed Drucilla and the others anticipated his interest. Omari didn't like that. Drucilla gestured to the seat.

"Please."

Omari sat then folded his arms across his chest. "Get on with it."

"Would you like something to drink?" Drucilla asked. "Beer? Palm wine? Nira juice?"

"No. I have a feeling I'll need my wits sharp for this conversation."

Drucilla nodded. "Then let's begin. We have a proposition for you. You are a mercenary, and Zahara vouches for your skills. If you do this, not only will you receive your stacks from the bank without tax, but we will double your amount and offer you a seat on the merchant council."

Omari knew what was coming next but decided to ask anyway.

"And what must I do to gain this windfall?"

Drucilla's eyes narrowed. "Kill Ogunsola."

Omari chuckled. "And how do you suppose I do that? I'm sure he's well protected."

"When has that ever stopped you?"

Another merchant stood. A silk turban covered her head, a matching veil hiding her face. The moment she began walking toward him Omari knew who she was. Joy coursed through his body as he stood and opened his arms. The woman smiled as she took off her veil and walked into his embrace. They hugged; their cheeks pressed against each other.

"Aisha," he whispered into her ear.

"Omari," she replied.

"Why the disguise?"

"I wanted to surprise you. I know how you like them."

Omari's hands began sliding downward and Aisha grabbed his wrists, moving them back to her waist.

"Careful. I'm a proper woman now."

"When has that ever been an issue?"

"Patience. Let's save your life first. And mine."

Omari let her go then stepped away. Aisha turned to face the council, and Omari admired the rear view.

"Omari asks a legitimate question," Aisha said. "Shall we tell him?"

Another merchant stood as Aisha took her seat. He was a short, heavily muscled, wide man with a halo of black and gray hair crowning his narrow head. His face was familiar.

"Yes, Ogunsola is well protected, more than any Grand Merchant before him and for good reason," the man said. "Although he has taken liberty with many of his traditional obligations, there is one that he cannot avoid, the daily market tour. From an hour after sunrise until an hour before sunset he must inspect the markets, sharing wisdom and settling disputes among the smaller merchants. The grand merchant compound is most vulnerable during this gap since most of his bodyguards are with him because of his unpopularity. That's when you can enter the compound."

"Merchant Amadou," Omari said. "I recognize you. You were Grand Merchant when I lived in the city. You served multiple terms. You know the compound very well."

The merchant smiled and nodded. "Welcome home, Omari. I remember when you left Sati-Baa. It was a scandalous situation. Aisha has vouched for you, and I trust her judgement."

Omari glanced at Aisha and winked. "So I assume I am to sneak into the compound then wait in hiding until Ogunsola and his entourage returns."

"There will be a few more mercenaries with you, including Zahara," Drucilla said.

"Why just send them?" Omari asked.

"Because none of them wear the ngisimaugi," Zahara said. "You have the best chance."

"The best chance of what, surviving?"

"Yes." Zahara stepped forward. "My sangoma senses tell me there is more to Ogunsola's behavior than greed. We may find more than what we're looking for."

"This sounds worse the more you explain it," Omari said. "I'm not the man for a one-way mission. I am not immortal."

"Neither are we," Aisha said. "We'll triple your offer."

Drucilla jerked her head toward Aisha. "What? No one agreed to that!"

"Be quiet, Drucilla," Aisha shot back. "I know this man very well. I know what it takes to deal with him."

Omari cursed himself silently. Aisha had him. She knew there was no way he would walk away from such a deal. The reward was definitely worth the risk.

"And what will you offer him next?" Amadou argued. "The title of Grand Merchant?"

"I have no interest in titles or positions," Omari said. "I no more wish to tell others what to do than I'm interested in doing what others want me to do. With one exception." Omari added the last words to placate Eda. "Three times my amount is reasonable. Add to that a serving house on the lakeshore and a fleet of fishing dhows and I'll do it."

"Done," Aisha said. The other merchants glared at her. "Our meeting is over. Feel free to return to your room. Please let me know if there is anything you need between now and the morning."

"I'd love to meet the people I'll be risking my life with," Omari said.

"That's been arranged. Thank you for accepting this task, Omari. Our lives are in your hands. You may leave."

Omari followed Zahara from the meeting room and back to his room.

"You know Merchant Aisha?" she asked.

"Yes," Omari replied. "You know the neighborhood I took you to?"

"Yes."

"It's her home as well."

Zahara's eyebrows rose. "You both have risen high."

"Apparently not high enough."

They reached his room.

"I could stay for a while," Zahara said. She had that look in her eyes which meant he wouldn't get much rest if she did.

"Not today," Omari replied.

Zahara looked disappointed.

"Do you know who will be coming with us?" he asked.

Zahara grinned. "I know of them." She left, closing the door behind her.

Omari sat on his bed, anticipating who would come soon. The door opened minutes later and Aisha entered. She closed the door, locked it, then ran to him and jumped into his waiting arms. For the second time since returning to Sati-Baa, tears filled his eyes. Aisha wept openly, her tears soaking his shoulder.

"I knew you weren't dead!" she said between sobs. "Not my Omari. Not you."

"I would never leave you alone," Omari replied.

Aisha kissed his forehead, his nose, his cheeks, and then his lips. They undressed each other then made love on top of the bedsheets. Afterwards they covered themselves then slept in each other's arms. A knock at the door woke them; Omari answered naked and was greeted by a shocked servant with a tray filled with food. Omari smirked as he took the tray and set in on the desk before closing and locking the door. Aisha sat up, pulling in her legs and wrapping her arms around them. Omari sat on the bed and kissed her knees.

"By the look of the food on that tray, I see you planned on being here," he said.

"I knew you wouldn't be sleeping alone," Aisha replied. "It was either me or Zahara."

Omari looked at her. "I don't know what you're talking about."

Aisha shoved his head playfully. "You can't lie to me, even after ten years apart. I saw it in her eyes every time she said your name."

"How do you feel about that?"

Aisha smiled. "The way I've always felt. We didn't belong to each other then and we don't now. Especially now. I don't know if you're the same person."

"Yet you slept with me. Am I?"

"Some things haven't changed. In fact, they've improved."

"I can say the same," Omari replied.

Aisha grabbed Omari by the back of the head and kissed him hard before getting out of bed. Omari watched her dress before doing the same. They sat on the bed and ate their meal, sharing old memories and filling each other in on their time apart. Aisha had met the son of a successful skins merchant and they married; the son inherited his father business not long after due his father's death. Aisha soon discovered the elder's death wasn't an accident; her husband had him killed when he discovered his father planned to sell the business instead of passing it on to him. Over time she learned why; her husband was as inept at business as his father was skilled and soon found himself owing too many creditors. He was killed in a dispute with collectors, who thought Aisha would be easy pickings once he was out of the way. They were wrong. After killing two of the collectors, she convinced the others to give her two moons to pay off the debt. She did, and with the leftover funds she'd earned she was able to return the business to success. It was the reason she was welcomed to the Merchant Council.

Omari captivated Aisha with his adventures, including his encounters with Eda. But it was the revelation of Nourbese which shocked her the most.

"A daughter!" Aisha laughed. "I always thought I'd be the first of us with a child, seeing I have the equipment for it."

"I can't say I was shocked," Omari admitted. "But I was surprised how I discovered it. Eda has plans, and I'm not sure I want to be a part of them."

"It's not like you have choice," Aisha said. "Our lives are not our own. The fates and the gods control all."

"I don't believe that," Omari said.

"After all you've been through, I think you would be the first to agree."

Omari pushed the tray aside and reached for Aisha. She shook her head and stood.

"It's almost time for you to meet the others," she said. "Zahara will be in charge. Do what she says and you might live."

"I'll do what has to be done," Omari replied.

Aisha sighed. "If that's so, then Eda help us."

"She always does."

Aisha left the room. Omari lay on his bed, savoring the time he's spent with Aisha. She'd risen high in Sati-Baa society and he wasn't surprised. She was the most intelligent person he'd ever met, and her beauty opened doors her personality couldn't budge. They often discussed how powerful they would be together, but knew they were even more effective apart. Life in the streets of Sati-Baa taught hard lessons, the most important being practical exceeded emotion every time.

It was evening when Zahara returned.

"The others are here. Come."

They went the opposite way from the meeting room down the hall to a flight of stairs that took them down two levels. It ended in a large storage area filled with crates and barrels. Omari followed Zahara past the inventory to an open area where a group of people talked. He grinned as he recognized the voices.

"I thought you'd be on the other side of Ki Khanga by now," Omari said.

Naya turned to him and shared a smile. "We almost were until Zahara sent us a homing dove."

Omari hugged the hamaria nahoda and shook wrists with Baraka, Khari, and Amri. Amri's face sported recent bruises.

"Did you win?" Omari asked.

"I always do," Amri replied, smiling and revealing a missing tooth.

Omari shook his head before speaking to Naya. "You know what we're supposed to do, right?"

Naya nodded. "Yes."

"And you came back anyway?"

Naya shrugged. "Life is risk. And this is a payoff you just can't walk away from. Besides, you're here, too."

"It seems we all have a death wish."

"Children of Daarila indeed," Baraka said.

"I don't know about this," Khari said.

"And yet you're here," Omari replied.

"Someone needs to look out for her," Khari said, nodding his head toward Naya.

"Don't blame me," Naya replied. "You're your own man."

"I'm your man," Khari said.

Zahara interrupted the small talk. "There are three more that will be joining us. They should be here soon."

"And who are they?" Omari asked.

"Merchant Drucilla's swords," Zahara replied. "Although I don't think they'll be much help."

"Spies?" Naya said.

"Most likely. They are from her personal guard, families that have served her family for generations. They are loyal, but not good fighters."

"Great," Omari said. "We can't even trust our own."

"They won't be a problem," Zahara said. "Just don't be near them when the fight happens."

Everyone nodded. Though Omari had not known the mahamaria for long, he'd fought with them and was confident of their skills.

Zahara waited until Drucilla's guards arrived before sharing her plan. She revealed a leather tube then took out and unrolled a parchment. Drawn on the parchment was a diagram of the Grand Merchant compound.

"I drew this map based on information from the merchants who have served as Grand Merchant and some of the former servants. It's as accurate as possible, but I'm sure there are some things missing.

"A coral stone wall surrounds the compound, wide enough for the guards to walk three abreast. The main compound is surrounded by a sprawling garden containing decorative ponds, trees, and flowers. The merchant's residence sits over it all, four stories rising high enough to be seen over the wall. Despite the modifications it's still a palace, not a fortress to be defended. Which was why Ogunsola filled the grounds with guards.

Zahara pointed at the rear of the compound. "We'll enter through servants' entrance. We bribed the latrine cleaner to let us join his crew.

"We have to clean the shitholes!?!" Khari exclaimed.

"Of course not," Zahara said. "But . . ."

"But what?" Omari asked.

"Once the cleaning is done, we'll have to remain in the latrine pit until nightfall."

Everyone groaned. Naya raised her hand.

"Please tell me we'll have some type of mask."

"We will, plus we'll have the potions the shit sweepers use to keep the odor bearable."

"Fragrant shit," Omari said. "Excellent."

Bakara raised his hand. "How will we know it's dark?"

"A drummer plays at dusk," Zahara replied. "As soon as we hear it, we move."

"Shouldn't we wait until the compound is settled?" one of Drucilla's guards asked.

"No," Zahara replied. "Once the house is secure Ogunsola will be unreachable. We rush to the upper level and get in his room before the doors are closed."

"Who is we?" Amir asked.

"Me and Omari. The rest of you will be stationed on the lower floors to make sure no one else comes up. Once the deed is done, we'll set the compound on fire and escape with other servants and guests."

Omari frowned. "Set the Grand Merchant compound on fire? Did the other merchants approve of this?"

Zahara smiled. "They don't know. But then they're not the ones risking their lives."

Drucilla's guards looked uncomfortable. Omari figured he would stay away from them.

"That's the plan," Zahara said. "Let's get some rest. Our day begins before sunrise tomorrow. May Eda be with us."

"May Eda be with us," everyone repeated.

They returned to the upper floor. Omari said his good nights then made his way to his room. Zahara caught up to him.

"Would you like some company?"

Omari smiled. "Do you have to ask?"

"Just wanted to make sure you weren't expecting anyone else."

"The night is ours," Omari said.

"Then let's not waste any time."

They entered his room then closed and locked the door.

* * *

"Wake up Omari. It's time."

Omari stirred and yawned. When he opened his eyes Zahara was dressed and armed. She glanced back at him and smiled.

"Hurry up. I'm going to gather the others. Meet me at the entrance."

Zahara left the room as Omari dressed. As he walked to the entrance a foul stench reached him. By the time he reached the doorway the smell was overpowering. The latrine cleaner's wagon was in the roundabout standing beside Zahara, the others gathered around. She greeted Omari with a head nod.

"Everyone, this is Kolle. He's taking us into the compound. He's risking his life for us, so pay attention."

Kolle stepped forward. "Ain't got much to say except don't fall into the latrine. You'll never wash away the smell."

Kolle went to the wagon and returned with the masks. Omari took his mask and secured it to his face. Although it didn't block the odor completely, it made it bearable. The mask was also a good disguise.

"Everyone put your weapons in the tool crate," Kolle said. "The guards never look inside."

Omari was reluctant to part with his swords and daggers but knew it was necessary. After they disarmed, they loaded the wagon and were on their way.

The sun was just breaking the horizon when they arrived at the compound gates. The guards did a quick inspection of the wagon, clearly disgusted by the smell. The gates opened and they traveled down the long cobblestone road to the compound. They veered to the right, following the road to the servants' entrance in the rear. The guards were walking away from the entrance before the wagon reached unloading. Omari leaned near the latrine cleaner.

"Don't they count your workers?"

"No, lucky for you," he replied. "They don't care how many people I bring, as long as the job is done."

"Not even on the way out?" Naya asked.

142

"Especially not then. We all smell like ass!" Kolle laughed and they laughed with him, thankful for a break in tension.

They unloaded the wagon quickly and entered the compound, following Kolle to the main sewer. Leaving the weapons bundle there, they did their duty, working their way upstairs to the toilets then working back to the main sewer. When they were done Kolle and his workers gathered their tools then began to leave.

"Eda be with you," he said to them. He left the main sewer and closed the door.

Omari and the others settled in to wait. Omari attempted to eat the sorghum he brought but scowled when the putrid taste of the sewer tainted his meal. It seemed to take forever when the evening drum sounded, vibrating the building. Everyone stood and armed themselves. Zahara went to the door and slowly opened it. She stepped out, then stuck her head back in.

"Let's go!"

They sprinted into the compound, Naya and the others taking their positions while Zahara and Omari bolted to the staircase. The sound of clashing swords rang behind them as he and Zahara rushed up to Ogunsola's room. They reached the long hallway as the guards were closing the doors. They were spotted; four guards ran for them, as two others continued to close the doors.

Omari took out his hand cannon. The element of surprise was gone so there was no need for stealth. He lit the fuse and the cannon blasted as the four guards reached them. All four collapsed, screaming in pain, their faces filled with metal shot. Omari and Zahara charged through the smoke toward the stunned door guards. Zahara reached the one on the right, slashing his shin before stabbing him in the gut. Omari took the guard on the left, decapitating him with a single slash. Zahara darted into the chamber, Omari close behind.

The chamber was empty with the exception of Ogunsola and two other figures. The Grand Merchant sat on his bed, still dressed in his finery from the market tour. The two figures standing beside him were familiar to Omari; they resembled the strange warriors he'd encountered in the Asanteman village and in Wadantu. This was more than just a greedy grand

143

merchant. Could Zahara's warnings about the Cleave be true? He stopped running, but Zahara continued to advance.

"Zahara, wait!" he shouted.

She ignored him. She ran to Ogunsola then stood before him. The others made no move toward her.

"Shit," Omari spat.

Zahara turned to face him, a smile on her face. "Sorry, Omari. The Ogunsola made me an offer I couldn't refuse. I'm sure the others are dead by now, and a force of constables are on their way to detain Aisha and the other merchants behind this scheme.

"So this was your plan all along?" Omari said.

Ogunsola stood. "It was my plan. I've been watching the council ever since I became Grand Merchant. I knew they would try to get rid of me as soon as they found someone brave enough or foolish enough to take their stacks. And then you came."

"My last task was to deliver you," Zahara said. "That, I have . . ."

Omari snatched a dagger from his belt and threw it in a flash. The blade hit Zahara in the throat with a force that knocked her back onto Ogunsola's bed. The Grand Merchant's eyes bucked with fear.

"Kill him!" he shouted.

The strange warriors advanced toward Omari, drawing their swords. Omari held out his arms in surrender.

"I don't know who you are or why you're after me, but I'm tired of running from you. It seems I am no match for Daarila."

Omari went to his knees. He took out his weapons and laid them on the floor. He then bowed his head.

"Make it quick," he said.

One of the warriors drew their swords and came. Omari peeked up and what he saw fascinated and terrified him. The sword blade shimmered with a blue light, meaning only one thing. It was made from pure kipande. How could they wield such a weapon without their ashé being drained? Omari realized then that Zahara did not serve the grand merchant; she served them.

The second warrior pushed Omari lower as the other raised his sword.

"Daarila's will be done," they said.

Omari backrolled to his knees then drew the dagger tucked in his pants on his back. He threw it into his executioner's cheek. The warrior howled as he dropped his sword and grabbed at the knife hilt protruding from his face. Omari dodged the other warrior's swing as he picked up his sword. No sooner did he raise it did the warrior's sword smash against it. His blade shattered, the metal cutting his face and his arms. The ngisimaugi flared as Omari scrambled away. He saw the dropped sword of the other warrior and dove for it. As his hands wrapped around the hilt, his body jolted. He was engulfed by the power of pure kipande. Omari waited for his life to end as the force consumed him, but that did not happen. Instead, an unexpected union forged between the blade and his tattoo. His wounds healed instantaneously; his body flooded by a feeling he'd never experienced before, a reservoir of what seemed like endless energy. He stood to face the warrior, whose puzzled expression made Omari smile.

"Now we're even," Omari said.

Omari attacked. He felt his body feeding off the kinpande's energy while the ngisimaugi protected him from harm. The warrior was skilled, but each blow between swords took its toll. Its guard slipped; Omari drove his blade into its stomach then ripped it out. The warrior fell to its knees then looked up into Omari's eyes. A smile slowly formed on its face.

"We will remember you."

Omari cut off its head. He stepped away from the warrior's body then let go of the tainted sword. His body jolted again and he fell on his ass.

"By the Cleave," he whispered.

"Omari!"

Omari turned to see Naya, Baraka, Khari, and one of Drucilla's guards enter the room. They stopped, gaping at the scene before them. Khari crept closer, staring at the bodies of the strange warriors.

"What is this?" he said.

"Something from the Cleave," Omari said. He struggled to his feet. Naya was at the foot of the bed looking at Zahara.

"This is your knife in her neck," she said.

"She betrayed us," Omari replied. "She was with them the entire time."

Omari looked around the room. "Where is Ogunsola?"

"Dead," Baraka said. "We were fleeing up the stairs from his guards when we met him escaping the chamber. Zara killed him before he could beg for his life. When the guards pursuing us saw him die, they turned and ran away."

"And Amri and the other guard?"

Naya lowered her eyes. "Dead."

"We have to get back to Aisha's compound," Omari said. "Zahara said the constables were sent to take her and the other merchants into custody."

"There's no rush," Naya replied. "If they were taken, the constables will bring them here. All we have to do is show them Ogunsola's corpse and they'll be freed."

"Let's go then," Omari said. "I've had enough of this place."

The others left the chamber to gather Ogunsola's remains. Omari started, then went to the kipande sword, the weapon glowing faintly on the stone. He went to the dead warrior, took the sheath, then returned to the sword. As he reached to pick up the weapon, he felt its pull, its attempt to link with him. Omari held the hilt long enough to put the weapon into its sheath. The pull dissipated. He did the same with the other sword, then draped them over his shoulders. Wherever they came from, they did not belong in the hands of normal Ki Khangans.

He joined the others at the compound steps. An hour later the constables arrived with the merchants and were shocked by what they saw. They quickly abandoned the merchants, galloping away on their horses. The merchants dismounted, their faces bright with joy. Drucilla's lone guard bowed to her and gave her a report; Aisha ran to Omari and kissed him.

"You didn't die," she said.

"You told me not to," he replied. "I always do what a beautiful woman tells me to."

Drucilla and her guard joined them.

"So Zahara betrayed us," she said.

Omari nodded. "And she paid for it. Now what of the promise you made to me?"

Drucilla frowned. "The promise Aisha made. It will be honored as soon as we select a new grand merchant."

"I think we should do it now," Omari said. "I've waited long enough to collect."

"I agree," Aisha said.

"Of course you would," Drucilla replied. "I will agree on one condition."

"What's that?" Aisha asked.

Drucilla smiled. "That you support my bid for Grand Merchant."

"Granted," Aisha replied.

Drucilla looked at Omari and he raised his hands.

"This has nothing to do with me," he said. "All I want is my stacks and my serving house."

"Then let us bring this to a close," Drucilla said.

"Indeed," Aisha said.

The merchants mounted their horses and together they left the compound. There was no one in the compound to see the latrine cleaner's wagon return. But this time the passengers were different, people dressed in strange clothing emitting a faint blue glow. They ignored the bodies on the compound grounds and within the building, bypassing them all until they reached the corpses of the pale warriors.

"Their swords!" one of the strange ones said. "We must find them!"

The other shook its head. "No time. We must take our own home. When we return, we'll have all the time in the world to find their swords. The wrath of Daarila awaits whoever possesses them."

* * *

Omari and fish monger glared at each other, both hugging a large basket of fresh spinfish.

"There is no way in the Cleave am I paying you two stacks for this!" Omari shouted.

"Fine!" Yenpape yelled back. "Then put it down! You will not steal from me today."

Omari cursed as he reached into his pouch and took out the stacks. "I hope you feel good about robbing an honest merchant."

Yenpape grinned as he took the stacks. "I would, if you were an honest merchant."

Omari took the basket. "Damn you to the Cleave, old man!" Yenpape's laughter grated on his nerves. He couldn't wait until his fishing dhows were complete and crewed. Dealing with thieves like Yenpape would be a bitter memory. As he made his way through the fish market his temper cooled. Life couldn't get much better. His payment from the Kamit scholars was finally in his hands and the merchants had honored their promise. The serving house given to him was in the perfect location, nestled between the docks and the city, and the docks for his fishing fleet directly across the road. He'd hired some of the best cooks in the city, paying them more than enough for their services.

Paki, his head cook, was waiting when he arrived. The sweaty round man took the basket from Omari and inspected it.

"This is a good batch," he said. "You have an eye for spinfish."

"Imagine when we get our own fleet," Omari replied. The entire city will be lined up at our doors!"

"Indeed!" Paki said. He took the basket to the back of the house to the kitchens. Omari inspected the serving house, making sure the palm wine, beer, and other libations were fully stocked for the night. He also inspected the hostel rooms, insuring each one was cleaned and prepared for guests. He was descending the stairs when he saw Aisha and her entourage enter. It had been weeks since he's seen her; both had been occupied with their professions. She was dressed resplendently as always; Omari wore a simple green tobe with white billowy pantaloons. His old Mikijen turban covered his braided head and a large medallion hung from his neck. At his waist was his new sword, the one he'd collected from the strange warrior he'd slain in the Grand Merchant compound. The other sword was hidden away, its location known only to him.

Omari greeted his old friend with customary respect. He knelt and touched his head to the ground before her feet. When he stood, Aisha frowned at him.

"That was totally unnecessary," she said.

"I thought of sprinkling my head with dust," he replied.

"You're so stupid. It looks like all is well."

"It is. Let me take you on a tour."

Omari greeted the others then led them through the serving house, outside into the kitchen and onto the new docks. They returned to the service house, where they sat as Omari's cook prepared a meal.

"This is nice," Aisha said. "But it could be so much more. You deserve it. With all you and I have been through, it's time we reaped the rewards fully. Are you sure you won't join the council?"

"I'm sure," Omari said. "Despite all this, I'm still a lucky street rat. You've always wanted more than me, and I'm glad you have it. But this is more than enough for me."

The servers arrived with their meals. Omari waited expectantly as everyone tasted their food. The nods and pleasant hums told him all he needed to know.

"This is delicious!" Aisha said. "Your cook is amazing. I might steal him from you."

"I'm sure Paki would love to cook for you, but he won't leave me. I pay him too much."

"We'll see about that." Aisha winked and Omari laughed.

They finished the meal, washing it down with palm wine. Afterwards Omari escorted Aisha and the others back to her wagon. Aisha pulled Omari aside as the others boarded.

"Tell me Omari, do you miss it?"

"Miss what?"

"The mercenary life. The travel, the danger, the adventure?"

"I can honestly say there was no point when someone was trying to stab me to death that I said, 'I wish I could do this forever!' I'm glad that's behind me now. It's better to share an adventure than to be in one."

Aisha broke decorum, kissing him passionately.

"Come see me," she said.

"I will."

"Soon."

"I will."

"I mean it."

"I do, too."

Aisha climbed into her coach then leaned out of the window. "I almost love you, Omari."

"I almost love you too, Aisha."

Aisha signaled the coach driver and they were on their way. Omari went inside to help prepare for the evenings business. The sun finally set on Sati-Baa and the Ngisimaugi came to life. Patrons filled the serving area as servers swirled between the tables. Djembe and kora players filled building with music, drowning out Paki's berating the kitchen staff. Omari wandered among the chaos, greeting customers, helping servers, and stopping now and then to play a game of oware or tell a lie or two. Omari was talking to two visitors from Mali when the moonlight shone through the entrance. He excused himself and went to the kitchen. Paki was waiting with a plate of spinfish and a gourd of palm wine. Omari took the meal and wine then made his way to his dock. A full moon rose over the lake, its light beam shining directly on the dock. He walked to the end of the boardwalk, placed the plate down, then raised the palm wine.

"To the ancestors who have watched over me." He poured the wine over the dock into the lake. He placed down the wine the picked up the plate. "To the lake spirits, for sharing your bounty." He emptied the plate into the lake then watched as the unseen denizens consumed his offering. Omari sat, took out his chagga pipe, and smoked. He was a few puffs in when he felt a comfort that had nothing to do with his pipe. He looked up to see Eda's silhouette in the moon.

"Welcome home, Omari Ket," she said, her voice coming from within him.

"Thank you for getting me here," Omari replied. "I hope you are done with me."

"For now."

Omari frowned. "There's more?"

Eda did not answer. He watched as her image faded away, leaving him alone with the moon. Omari shrugged and continued smoking. There was nothing he could do when it came to the whims of a goddess. He could only embrace the moment he was in as he always had. The past had passed. The present was present. The future kept its secrets.

Omari finished his smoke. He picked up the plate and gourd, then sauntered down the dock to the serving house.

-End-

Afterword

And so Omari Ket's adventures have come to an end. But that's not the end of Omari Ket. As Aisha said, *Our lives are not our own. The fates and the gods control all.*' So what to the gods have in store for Omari? Eda only knows.

I'd like to thank everyone who has taken this journey with me. Thank you for talking me into 'sparing' Omari from his original fate. If not for you, these stories would never have been written. I hope you will continue to journey with us as we share more stories from world of Ki Khanga. Be Eda Blessed.

ABOUT THE AUTHOR

Milton J. Davis is an acclaimed Black speculative fiction author and the founder of MVmedia, LLC, an independent publishing company based in Atlanta, Georgia. MVmedia specializes in science fiction, fantasy, and sword-and-soul narratives that draw inspiration from African and African Diaspora cultures, histories, and traditions. Davis has penned over thirty novels and short story collections, including *Changa's Safari*, *Woman of the Woods*, *Amber, and the Hidden City*, and *Muscadine Wine*. His work spans genres such as sword-and-soul, science fiction, and fantasy. He has co-edited several influential anthologies, such as *Griots: A Sword and Soul Anthology* and *Griots: Sisters of the Spear*, alongside Charles R. Saunders. He has also worked on *Steamfunk! Dieselfunk,* and *The Ki Khanga Anthology* and *Dieselfunk!* with Balogun Ojetade. These collections have played a pivotal role in shaping the sword-and-soul subgenre. Davis's short stories have been featured in prestigious publications, including *Black Panther: Tales of Wakanda*, *Slay: Stories of the Vampire Noire*, and *Obsidian: Literature in the African Diaspora*. His story "The Swarm" was nominated for the 2017 British Science Fiction Association Award for Short Fiction, and "Carnival" received a nomination in 2020. In 2022, Davis was honored with the East Coast Black Age of Comics Convention

Pioneer Lifetime Achievement Award, recognizing his significant contributions to Black speculative fiction. In 2024, he received the ConCarolinas Polaris Award, and the DeepSouth Con Phoenix Award for his contributions to Southern fandom.

For more adventures from the land of Ki Khanga, visit us at www.mvmediaatl.com!